The

826

Quarterly

The

826

Quarterly

[*Published twice yearly at least*]

VOLUME 3 • SUMMER 2004

An 826 Valencia original,
published September 2004,
as the third edition of the 826 Quarterly.
Created by all hands on deck at 826 Valencia.
www.826valencia.org

Special thanks to:
The Pirate Store at 826 Valencia
www.826valencia.org/store

Special editorial attention was provided by
Margaret Berry, Renata Ewing, Taylor Jacobson,
Leslie LaDow, Monica Maduro, Melanie Mah, Abner Morales,
Amie Nenninger, Brigid O'Neil, Pavla Popovich, Rachael Richardson,
Karen Schaser, and Anna Ura.
Production by Alanna Hale and Anna Ura.
Book design by Alvaro Villanueva.

ISBN: 1-932416-30-7

Printed in Canada by WestCan P.G.

To Timmy,
the boy in the window,
because you share your visions with us.

Contents

Foreword

Not long ago—just two years ago, in fact—San Francisco was a city without a pirate store. Itinerant pirates, having landed upon these shores, could wander the streets for weeks without finding a source for replacement mop heads, boots, rope, bottles, lard, quill pens, black hats, glass eyes (or eye patches, for the more modest). Nowhere could a shore-bound pirate sit in a darkened mini-theater to watch fish swim; nowhere could he find low-cost white shirts or mysterious wooden boxes.

No longer. In April of 2002, a few visionaries opened a pirate store at 826 Valencia, and now all buccaneers have a place to replenish their supplies when they reach San Francisco. Among the more daring pirates who have visited 826, a few have been brave enough to pass beyond the chain that divides the store from its alter-ego: 826 Valencia, a writing center. Those who have made their way into that cozy, wood-floored, bookcase-walled space may have seen students between the ages of eight and eighteen writing stories, poems, screenplays, and comic books. They may have encountered second-graders on a field trip, working with professional writers and illustrators to make bound storybooks. They may have met students from Galileo High School writing their college application essays—honing their sentences, making lists of what they might contribute to their prospective schools, and finding ways to communicate their individual strengths and achievements. They might have encountered the forbidding-yet-story-loving Mister Blue, who lives in a loft above the writing center, and whose wrath can only be appeased by regular deliveries of young writers' work.

When 826 Valencia first opened its doors, some people questioned the wisdom of locating a tutoring center in such close proximity to a pirate store, given the well-known fact that children are pirates' third-favorite food (after hardtack and salt cod). Now that the tutoring center has been open for nearly two years, Bay Area experts have conceded that the location of the pirate store has not, in fact, proved dangerous to children. In fact, no child has been known to have been eaten as of yet. Instead, young people are present at 826 in record numbers, and the work they produce has delighted and astounded readers across the country. During one of my tutoring visits, a sixth-grader wrote about his red Lamborghini, which came equipped with a pizza oven in the glove-box. Another described his family's emigration from Brazil; he wrote about the terrifying thrill of flying over the ocean for the first time, with nothing beneath him but thousands of feet of air and miles of glittering waves. In the pages of this quarterly you'll read the work of young writers like Kate Mehl, who tells us where to find a poem; Marieke Thomas, who looks a gift horse in the mouth; and Kira Deutch, whose describes the painful flirtation of the sun through tree branches. In a heartbreaking story by Teresa Cotsirilos, you'll meet Goose, the tiny jade-eyed friend of a girl whose mother is dying; in Amelia Rosenman's work, you'll learn what can be done with a book of Pablo Neruda poems, a deck of playing cards, white paper, rubber cement, a pen, and the desire to become a maker of small miracles.

And speaking of miracles, who would have imagined that an idea like 826 Valencia—a writing center that runs entirely on the goodwill of volunteers, the generosity of donors, and the desire of urban children to study writing—would succeed so profoundly and have such a strong impact upon a community? Hundreds of volunteers have offered their services to the program; more are always needed. And 826 is not just a San Francisco phenomenon, as it turns out; thanks to the work of hundreds of New York residents, 826NYC has opened its doors. I have a feeling that these two locations are just the beginning. The pirates who have visited 826 are going out and spreading the word across the world. Instead of eating young people, they are reading them.

Now, if you dare, you may turn the page and do the same.

—*Julie Orringer*

The Staff and Volunteers of 826 Valencia

Staff:

Nínive Calegari, Executive Director

Dave Eggers, Founder and Teacher

Yosh Han, Purveyor of Pirate Supplies/Events Producer

Tracy Barreiro, Finance Manager

Erin Neeley, Volunteer Coordinator

Susan Tu, Programs Assistant

Phil Roh, Programs Assistant, In-Schools Program Coordinator

Alvaro Villanueva, Design and Publishing Director

Julia White, 826 National Coordinator

Volunteers, Tutors, Interns, and Workshop Teachers:

Cat Aboudara, Nathan Adachi, Mike Adamick, Nyla Bialek Adams, Mika Akutsu, Pat Allbee, Michelle Allison, Christina Amini, Lessley Anderson, Tom Annese, John Aranda, Andrea Arata, Jessica Arndt, Gina Arnold, Ellen Atkinson, Sally Baggett, Leslie Bahr, Maria Baird, Monya Baker, Wendy Baker, Gina Balibrera, Gabriela Barragan, Nicky Batill, Jessica Baxter, Kevin Bayley, Colleen Bazdaric, Neva Beach, Rebecca Beal, Dana Beatty, Jim Beckmeyer, Devon Beddard, Jordan Benjamin, Michael Berger, Debra Berliner, Marcella Bennhard, Margaret Berry, Jason Biehl, Jessica Binder, Elizabeth Binyon, Jennifer Birch, Jenny Bitner, Joni Blecher, Steve Blumenthal, Ran Bolton, Charles Boodman, Amick Boone, Kelly Booth, John Borland, James Borda, Karen Boudreaux, Bee Bradley, Rachel Brahinsky, Nathan Bransford, Ben Brewer, Thomas Brierly, Sara Bright, Kiara Brinkman, Roxanne Brodeur, Po Bronson, Lisa Brown, Nicole Brown, Leora Broydo Vestel, Lee Bruno, Pamela Burdak, Sarah Burgundy, Ben Burke, Natalie Burke, Christina Caamano, Patricia Callahan, Aboudana Cana, Paul Caparotta, Carin Capolongo, Caryn Cardello, Sandra Cardoza, Pamela Carl, William Carlsen, Michelle Carter, Michele Casale, Michael Case, Jessica Castillo, Michael Cavanaugh, Halsey Chait, Rachel Chalmers, Melissa Chamberlin, Amelie Charnaux, Evan Chase, Ana Chavier, Jill Checker, George Chen, Ie-chen Cheng, Sam Chennault, Pam Chernoff, Marianna Cherry, Gretchen Chesley, Michael Ching, David Chow, Lindsey Chow, Ella Christoph, Scott Christopher, Nick Cimiluca, Kim Clark, Kevin Cline, Shannon Clouston, Chloe Cockburn, Kit Cody, Meryl Cohen, Mary Colgan, Chris Colin, Caiti Collins, Jennifer Cook, Martha Cooley, Sara Coppin, Elizabeth Corbus, John Cornwell, Annie Correal, Julia Cosgrove, Malaika Costello-Dougherty, Teresa Cotsirilos, Mary Ann Cotter, Annie Countryman, Katherine Covell, Caitlin Craven, Ryan Crawford, Kirk Crippens, Spencer Cronk, Gregory Crouch, Yvette

Cuenco, Kevin Cummins, Bobby Cupp, Kevin Curran, Bekah Cutler, Jane Cutler, James Daly, Kristen Daniel, Erik Davis, Jaina Davis, Julie Davis, Meara Day, Lauren De Bruyn, Ashia De la Bastide, Mark De la Vina, Maria De Lorenzo, Solidad Decosta, Lisa Degliantoni, James Dekker, Lisa Marie Delgadillo, Tracy Deluca, Sara Deneweth, Kenwyn Derby, Corina Derman, Calla Devlin, Christine Dibiasi, Eva Dienel, Isaac Dietz, Stefanie DiLibero, Russell Dillon, Cory Doctorow, Kathleen Dodge, Shannon Dodge, Jans Donald, Amy Donsky, Denise Dooley, John Douglass, Norman Doyle, Marie Drennan, Marcie Dresbaugh, Eric Dumbleton, Jessica Dur, Leila Easa, Grace Ebron, Issac Ebersole, Katie Edmonds, Gail Edwards, Shirley Edwards, Cindy Ehrlich, Amanda Eicher, Eve Ekman, Steve Elliot, Geoffrey Ellis, Diana Elrod, Christina Empedodes, Gloria Eng, Erin English, Lee Epstein, Cindy Erlich, Carlo Espinas, Denise Esteves, Starla Estrada, Barry Ettenger, Brian Eule, Kasey Evans, Ted Everson, Renata Ewing, Max Farber, Tyler Farmer, Katie Farnsworth, Andrea Feddersen, Deborah Fedorchuk, Mandy Field, Peter Finch, Linda Finocchiaro, Brittany Fiore-Silfvast, Jamie Flam, Mark Follman, Sarah Fontaine, Chantal Forfota, Ilona M. Fox, Laura Fraenza, Alex Frankel, Katie Fraser, Wendy Freedman, Luke Fretwell, Milli Frisbie, Tanya Gallardo, Christi Gambill, Elizabeth Gannes, Erin Gardner, Julia Garson, Heather Gates, Sarah Gault, Emanuela Gavanzla, Lizi Geballe, Malka Geffen, Beth Gerber, Samay Gheewala, Antonia Giannoccaro, Alex Giardino, John Gibler, Alison Gilbert, Rod Gilchrist, Michael Ginther, Debra Glass, Julia Glassman, Jenny Glennon, Lianna Glodt, Robert Glushko, Aimee Goggins, Lis Goldschmidt, Rachel Goldstein, West Gomez, Anastasia Goodstein, Linda Goossens, Eric Gottesman, Michalle Gould, Jason Grace, Melissa Graeber, Ben Graham, Ryan Gray, Josh Green, Matthew Green, Mari Greenberg, Josh Greene, Lauren Groff, Cristal Guderjahn, Tim Gunderson, Janet Guthrie, Leslie Guttman, Alanna Hale, Holly Hale, Jim Haljun, Tika Hall, Wesley Hall, Lane Halley, Lauren Halsted, Ethan Halter, Leslie Hamanaka, Cary Hammer, Christian Hanlon, Elizabeth Hanson, Howard Harband, Reyhan Harmanci, Josh Harnden, Leslie Harpold, Jim Harrington, Tania Harry, Sarah Haufrect, Noah Hawley, Casey Haymes, Tracey Haynes, Clane Hayward, Maya Hazarika, Carol Hazenfield, Jason Headley, Terrance Heath, Micaela Heekin, Audrey Helderman, Eric Hellweg, Nicole Henares, Stacey Hendren, Leslie Henkel, Kathleen Hennessy, Mario Henriquez, Steve Hermanos, Andy Hess, Justin Hibbard, Denis Higginbotham, Meg Hilgartner, Wendy Hill, Elizabeth Hille, Emily Hitz, Luke Hogan, Elizabeth Hollander, Jim Hollingsworth, Matthew Honan, Andro Hsu, Pem Huddleston, Bree Humphries, Annie Hunt, Peter Huppert, Elizabeth Hurt, Robert Ingall, Angela Ingel, Mari Jack, June Jackson, Abigail Jacobs, Taylor Jacobson, Maggie Jacobstein, Peter Jacoby, Donald Jans, Gail Jardine, Arne Johnson, Cindy Johnson, Ellen Johnson, Andy Jones, Gerard Jones, Stanley Jones, Matt Joyce, Jessica Kahn, John Kane, Joshua Kamler, Emily Kaplan, Tilda Kapuya, Monica Karaba, Lindsay Keach, Sarah Keefe, Helena Keeffe, Lindsey Keenan, Aliah Kelly, Leslie Kelly, Ricky Kelly, Christina Kelso, Deborah Kelson, Rosemary Kendrick, Elizabeth Kennedy, Evan Kennedy, Christina Kerby, Jon Kiefer, Jumin Kim, Tae Kim, Kristi Kimball, Alison King, Jennifer King, Martha Kinney, Alison Kip, Ginevra Kirkland, Daniel Kirkeby, Susanna Kittredge, Shari

Kizirian, Stephanie Klein, Kim Klover, Lindsay Knisely, Conan Knoll, Rodney Koeneke, Lee Konstantinou, Charles Koppelman, Susie Kramer, Caroline Kraus, Kate Kudirka, Adrian Kudler, Peter Kupfer, Nick Kwaan, Adrienne LaBonte, Nina Lacour, Leslie Ladow, William Laven, Linda Lagunas, Sarah Lahey, Jennee LaMarque, Ryan Lambert, Julie Landry, Adam Lane, Halley Lane, Elliott Lange, Chad Lange, Kim Latford, Devorah Lauter, Jeremey Lavoi, Doug Lawrence, Galen Leach, Shelly Leachman, Marc Leandro, Kevin Lee, Lisa Lee, Sarah Lefton, Joel Leimer, Krystine Leja, Chad LeJeune, Jacynth LeMaistre, Chad Lent, Amanda Leoal, Shari Leskowitz, Scott Levine, Shira Levine, John Levitt, Kenya Lewis, Kristina Lewis, Gideon Lewis-Kraus, Karen Lichtenberg, Sarah Lidgus, Elyse Lightman, Natalie Linden, Andrew Lipnick, Seth Liss, Megan Lisska, Dennise Lite, Candice Liu, Julie Liu, Lily Livingston, Colleen Lloyd, Jesse Loesberg, Laurie Loftus, Grace Loh, Celine Lombardi, Joanne Long, David Looby, Pat Lovitt, Amber Lowi, Huy Luong, Alexis Lynch, Dantia MacDonald, Hollie Mack, Kyle Mack, Monica Maduro, Kim Magowan, Melanie Mah, Aimee Male, Sara Mann, Benny Maraget, Peter Marcus, Bernhard Marcella, Scott Marengo, Ann Marino, Hedia Maron, Frank Marquardt, Megan Martin, Mariana Martinez, Amie Marvel, Mike Mason, Noah Mass, John Maxey, Julie Mayhew, Kristin Mayville, Brie Mazurek, Michael McAllister, Taryn McCabe, Sara McClelland, Jonathon McLeod, Laura McClure, Kate McDonough, Nancy McGee, Lorien McKenna, Robert McLaughlin, Heather McMurphy, John McMurtrie, Frederick Mead, Allegra Medsen, Sierra Melcher, Sarah Melikian, Heidi Meredith, Robert Merryman, Carol Mersey, Ezra Mersey, Matthew Micari, Erika Mielke, Aaron Miller, Nicole Miller, Ryan Miller, Salome Milstead, Berry Minott, Logan Mirto, Greta Mittner, Jennifer Moffit, Elizabeth Montalbano, Sara Moore, Annie Marie Moore, Ana Moraga, Abner Morales, Lindsey Moreland, Mathew Morgan, Samantha Morgan, Megan Motrin, A. Moxee, Amelia Mularz, Rachel Mulchrone, Nish Nadaraja, Uno Nam, Alysha Naples, Amanda Navone, Sheila Nazzaro, Erin Ann Neeley, Ali Neff, Jennifer Nellis, Anne Nelson, Amie Nenninger, Emberly Nesbitt, Matt Ness, Laurel Newby, Kate Nicolai, Jennifer Nicoloff, Monica Norton, Nina Nowack, Risa Nye, Lori Nygaard, Colleen O'Connor, Amiee O'Donnell, Ryan O'Donnell, Jeff O'Leary, Nada O'Neal, Anna O'Neil, Brigid O'Neil, Leila O'Neil, Beth O'Rourke, Antonia Oakley, Rebecca Oksner, Kathryn Olney, Nick Olsson, Edward Opton, Kelly Osterling, Owen Otto, Veronica Padilla, Jeremy Padow, Patty Page, Jessica Pallington, Denny Palmer, Jeni Paltiel, Alaine Panitch, Christina Papanestor, Jen Park, Dilaria Parry, Matt Parsons, Jessica Partch, Robert Pasquini, Jill Passano, David Pava, Kate Pavao, Jesse Pearson, Tenny Pearson, Matt Perault, Andrew Peters, Charlotte Petersen, Kate Petty, Mary Petrosky, Gavin Pherson, Sue Pierce, Susan Pike, Micah Pilkington, Gregory Pleshaw, Melissa Pocek, Shelby Polakoff, Paula Ponsetto, Pavla Popovich, Jason Porter, Jeff Porter, Daria Portillo, Miriam Posner, Todd Pound, Peter Prato, Gabrielle Prendergast, Tara Prescott, Marin Preske, Jenny Prichett, Carolyn Pritchard, Dina Pugh, Conan Putnam, Yenie Ra, Naomi Raddatz, Louise Rafkin, Kismet Ragab, Daniel Ralston, Rolando Ramirez, Abby Ramsden, Suneel Ratan, Julie Ratner, Richard Raucci, Jane Rauckhorst, Arena Reed, Megan Reed, Kazz Regelman, Dalia Regos, Ariana

Reguzzoni, Rachael Reiley, Jennifer Reimer, Ken Reisman, Cathy Remick, Sarah Rich, Joel Richards, David Richardson, Rachel Richardson, Tina Richardson, Nicki Richensin, Michelle Richmond, Matt Ridella, Maria Riley, Ashley Rindsberg, Jen Rios, Kristina Rizga, Jen Robb, Becka Robbins, Jason Roberts, Blake Robin, James Rocchi, Katherine Rochemont, Patrick Rock, Brian W. Rogers, Sage Romano, Gabriel Roth, Meika Rouda, Allison Rowland, Glendon Roy, Danielle Rubi, Shari Rubin, Paul Rueckhaus, Lisa Ruff, Christina Ruiz-Esparanza, Catalina Ruiz-Healy, Margo Rusovick, Chris Ryan, Dana Sacchetti, Sarahjane Sacchetti, Shirazi Sahar, Brynn Saito, Azmeer Salleh, Eleanor Sananman, Victoria Sanchez, Jessica Sanfilippo, Sara Sani, Gianmarco Savio, Abigail Sawyer, Laura Schadler, Mary Schaefer, Brett Schaeffer, Karen Schaser, Deborah Schatten, Sydney Schaub, Darrell Scheidegger, Kevin Schindler, Kellie Schmitt, Samantha Schoech, Gregg Schoenberg, Seth Schoenfeld, Tracy Seeley, Laura Scholes, Charles Schoonover, Alyssa Schwartz, Ana Schwartzman, John Scopelleti, Gil Sectzer, Tetine Sentell, P. Segal, Ashley Sferro, Rebecca Shapiro, Sudeep Sharma, Elaine Shen, Becca Sherman, Vaughn Shields, George Shultz, Sam Silverstein, Catherine Silvestre, Matt Simon, Roderick Simpson, Saurabhi Singh, Andy Slater, Julia Smith, Karen Smith, Pamela Jean Smith, Robert Solley, Jennifer Sonderby, Eleni Sotos, Lavinia Spalding, B. June Speaker, Eric Spitznagel, Libby Spotts, Charlene St. John, Jane St. John, Sandra Staklis, Lesley Stampleman, Clifford Stanley, Joy Stanley, Claire Stapleton, Jill Stauffer, Tabitha Steager, Marla Stener, Jon Stenzler, Marisa Stertz, Aaron Stewart, Ian Stewart, Jeannine Stickle, Emily Stoddard, Rebecca Stoddard, Dusty Stokes, Sarah Stone, Jeanne Storck, Alice Stribling, Andrew, Strickman, Andrew Strombeck, Evan Stubblefield, Harold Stusnick, Mo Stz, Eileen Sugai, Jon Sung, Danica Suskin, Christy Susman, Anne Swan, Elizabeth Switaj, Andrew Swyak, Caitlin Talbot, Philippe Tapon, Cheryl Taruc, Sandra Tavel, Leslie Tebbe, Krissy Teegerstrom, Alex Tenorio, Justin Tenuto, David Thal, Arul Thangavel, John Theisen, Evany Thomas, Jason Thompson, Jennifer Thompson, Rob Thomson, Kris Thorig, Thomas Thornhill, Heather Tidgewell, Rob Tocalino, Jennifer Tomaro, Chris Tong, Danny Torres, Zoe Torres, Andy Touhy, Jennifer, Traig, Cary Troy, Alyssa Tsukako, Susan Tu, Susan Tunis, Jason Turbow, Andrea Turner, Anna Ura, Phoebe Vaughan, Chloe Veltman, Vendela Vida, Michelle Vizinau-Kvernes, Rafael Vranizan, Bonnie Wach, Andrew Wagner, Maria Walcutt, Elizabeth Wang, Ethan Watters, Lisa Webster, Toni Weingarten, Joshua Wein, Carol Weinstein, Jeffrey Weinstock, Gabe Weisert, Greta Weiss, Jennifer Wells, Amelie Wen, Jess Wendover, Joe Werth, Amber West, Pamela Weymouth, Christine Whalen, Aaron White, Alison Wiener, Eric Wilinski, Doug Wilkins, Camille Williams, Moira Williams, Sean Williford, Cabala Winble, Charles Wincorn, Elizabeth Wing, Emily Wittman, Sasha Wizansky, Andy Wong, Grace Wong, Liz Worthy, Cynthia Wood, Lyn Woodward, Jennifer Wright-Cook, Jenny Wu, Sinclair Wu, Wendy Wu, Ed Yoon, Matthew Yeoman, Gene Yuson, Liane Ykoff, Elizabeth Zambelli, Susie Zavala, Mimi Zeiger, Kim Zetter, Fritz Zuhl, Todd Zuniga.

826 Valencia Programs Overview

We are able to offer all of our student programs free of charge because of the large number of volunteers that participate with 826 Valencia.

ONE-ON-ONE TUTORING

Five days a week, 826 Valencia is packed with students who come in for free, one-on-one, drop-in tutoring. Some students need help with homework. Others come in to work on more ambitious extra-curricular projects such as novels and plays. 826 Valencia accommodates students of all skill levels and interests, from the severely dyslexic, to the autistic, to the unusually gifted. We're particularly proud of our thriving services for young students learning English.

WORKSHOPS

826 Valencia also offers free workshops that provide in-depth instruction in a variety of areas that schools don't often include in their curriculum. We've had workshops on writing college-entrance essays and on writing comic books, on preparing for the SAT, on learning software programs, and on producing films. All of the workshops are taught by working professionals and are limited in size, so students get plenty of individual attention.

FIELD TRIPS

Three or four times a week, 826 Valencia welcomes an entire class for a morning of high-energy learning. Classes can request a custom-designed curriculum on a subject they've been studying, such as playwriting, or choose from one of our five field trip plans. The most popular is the Storytelling & Bookmaking Workshop. In two hours, the students write, illustrate, publish, and bind their own books. They leave with keepsake books and a newfound excitement for writing. Other field trips allow students to meet a local author, to learn the basics of journalism, or to work on a student publication.

IN-SCHOOLS PROGRAM

Because it is sometimes infeasible for classes to come to 826 Valencia, tutors go to them. We dispatch teams of volunteers who go to local schools and help classes work on various projects. 826 Valencia has helped students with their college application essays at Raoul Wallenberg High School, Thurgood Marshall Academic High School, and the School of the Arts, among others. Tutors have helped students create Peanut Journeys (which are creative stories about an adventurous peanut) at Guadalupe Elementary School. They've spent a month working intensively on writing with the students of Grattan Elementary, and five months with the students of Galileo High. Recently they helped juniors and seniors at Thurgood Marshall Academic High School to publish their own book, which we sell in our store to benefit our programs.

Our first ever full time, in-school project reached a successful conclusion with the close of this past school year. The students at Everett Middle School worked year round with 826 tutors in a classroom we had turned into a pirate-themed lab to research, write, and perfect their English and history assignments. The Everett Writers' Room was site to much tutoring—in fact, every single student at Everett was tutored. The Writers' Room also held the offices of the *Straight-Up News*, the school's student-published newspaper, and class-wide projects. As a final project, the eighth grade social studies class took on the persona of an early twentieth-century muckraker and created a persuasive "social issue" pamphlet.

STUDENT PUBLICATIONS

826 Valencia currently produces a plethora of publications, each of which contains work done by students in our various programs, and is put together primarily by the students themselves, in collaboration with professional publishers. These projects represent some of the most exciting work at 826 Valencia, as they expose and enable Bay Area students to an experience a level of control over their written

work otherwise not available to them. 826 Valencia students put out the following publications:

In our latest anthology project teaming 826 Valencia volunteers with a local high school, *Waiting to be Heard: Youth Speak Out about Inheriting a Violent World*, thirty-nine students from San Francisco's Thurgood Marshall Academic High School write about the themes of violence and peace, through perspectives that are personal, local, and global. With a foreword by Isabel Allende, the book combines essays, fiction, poetry, and experimental writing pieces to create a passionate collection of student voices.

Talking Back: What Students Know about Teaching is a completely student-produced 140-page paperback book which, in the words of the students, "delivers the voices of the class of 2004 from Leadership High School. In reading this book, currently being used as a required reading textbook at California State University San Francisco, you will understand the relationships students want with their teachers, how students view classroom life, and how the world affects students."

The 826 Quarterly (Volume 3 of which is in your hands at this moment) is put out at least twice a year with writing submitted by youth from all over the San Francisco Bay Area. To submit a story, a poem, a play, or any form of writing you feel would be suitable for publication, please write to quarterly@826valencia.com with your piece attached. Please be sure to include your full name, age, school, and any other pertinent information.

We also publish scores of chapbooks each year. These are collections of writing from our workshops, in-school projects, and class projects from schools that team up with us. This year, our most popular titles include: *A Poem for Each Blade of Grass, The Fifth Grade Tiny Tigers' Literary Magazine, Glass Over Dynamite, A Poem Is Worth a Thousand Pictures,* and the *Griot Girlz: Girl Scout Write-On Program* book.

Workshops

Workshops happen most every day at the 826 Valencia writing lab, even on weekends. Our workshops are taught, free of charge, by professionals working in the field, and cover very specific topics to develop every writing technique young people might need or wish to develop. There are artistic workshops that teach all the forms of fiction, poetry, and non-fiction; there are practical workshops that help kids write arguments to persuade their parents, and college-bound seniors write their application statements. There are also trade related workshops that teach how to write songs, magazine articles, and comic books. Some of the students and teachers of these workshops, as a whole class, submit to the *826 Quarterly* the writing they have produced, which we are glad to share with you.

But keep in mind, as great as the pieces you are about to read are, they only represent a small portion of the total work produced by 826 workshop authors. Of the scores of topics we want to publish, we are limited by space to include only the following workshops' submissions.

EXPERIMENTAL FICTION

[*This workshop, taught by Julia Glassman, sought to introduce students ages four-teen to eighteen to new and unusual methods of storytelling. The students disguised their stories in different forms, explored their characters' thoughts through stream of consciousness, and even tried their hands at William Burroughs' cut-up technique, along with other exercises and prompts.*]

Wanted: Missing Wife

by AMELIA ROSENBAUM

Age 17, Lick-Wilmerding High School

WANTED:
Missing wife. Anna-Margaret Stevenson, possibly May or Maggie. Soft Modigliani chin, knitted blue sweater, eyes like dark cherries.

MISSING SINCE:
12 September, noon. Suicide, murder or sexual affair—all unlikely. Probable basket case.

NOT A LIKELY ABDUCTION:
Low stakes. Not eye-catching. Hat-wearer. Childless. No motivation apparent.

SUSPECTED CAUSES AND EVIDENCE:
1. Consistently impersonal mail, e.g., bills, Sara Lee advertise-ments, Safeway coupons, insincere Christmas card from Democratic Party.
2. Devastatingly clean kitchen, smirking bottles of Pride and Joy, glinting faucet, obedient toaster.

3. Silent unkindnesses of husband, e.g., intimidating eyeglasses, kisses that miss the face, his thumb caressing pages of important green book.
4. General lack of whistling or briskness.

LAST REPORTED:
Legs shaking in kitchen chair. Twisting ring around little finger. Fragile, furious. "What was it you said about the bench and the sidewalk chalk and the little one in a pink sweatshirt and her fingers like little tubes of honey? Will I always wince when I see perfect, little, white teeth; will I?"

EXPECTED DESTINATIONS:
Florence, the park on Grant, farmer's market (the strawberry woman), florist's, spice aisle of upscale grocery, public library, cemetery, imaginary forest.

NOTES:
Dazed lady reported at Grand Hotel, fits description, found lost on top floor gaping at flower arrangement for upcoming wedding. Carries purse with lipstick; wears small beads, plastic ring with yellow rose painted on (junk), wool scarf, silver high heels. Has settled on couch in lobby. Rubs feet occasionally. Stares at revolving door.

[*This workshop, taught by Julia Glassman, sought to introduce students ages four-teen to eighteen to new and unusual methods of storytelling. The students disguised their stories in different forms, explored their characters' thoughts through stream of consciousness, and even tried their hands at William Burroughs' cut-up technique, along with other exercises and prompts.*]

Girl at a Bus Stop

by JULIANA FRIEND
Age 15, Lick-Wilmerding High School

I'd seen her so many times before, maybe even every day. Or if I hadn't, I remembered her nearly as often. Every afternoon at around three, her puffy white jacket would be sitting there, wrapping her up tight as she waited for the bus to come. One January day I first noticed the stain—a big wine-colored splotch that ruined the perfect whipped-up egg froth that had hidden her for so long. Whoever had spilled the wine had been very, very sorry. The second it happened they'd bent over to where she had lain draped on the couch, and they'd soaked the wine up with mounds of paper towels. Their eyes had darted between the red monster growing bigger and bigger and the girl's face sinking lower and lower into the pillow. For a couple of hours they had spoken tensely, if they needed to speak to each other at all. But this had ceased soon enough. From deeper inside them, sense and love had surfaced again, and they had embraced in a tacit apology. That same January day the bus had eventually pulled up and taken her away. A minute later I left the bus stop and walked home.

I had forgotten my key, and it was a Tuesday, so Marge (my mother), would have had the garage combination changed again. She was a secretary who organized both her life and mine into orderly piles. When she had seen a man rummaging through our garbage can, she had quickly filed him away into the overwhelmingly large pile reserved for unpredictability. Since then, every Tuesday the combination had changed in order to "hold the treachery at bay." In any case, I sat myself down on the cold cement steps and began the long Tuesday wait. I began to think about what the girl was doing now.

I thought, as I am waiting impatiently, she is probably just reaching her destination, a pawnshop this time. She is turning the knob and stepping over the threshold. The acrid smell is colliding with her nostrils and she hacks into her sleeve (so as not to spread germs). Her neck is twisting right and left and right again as she examines the small, unlit room. No one is at the counter, so she bides time by wandering around a bit, unwilling to disturb the owner of the shop who, as she imagines, must be occupied. She aimlessly passes by the dusty electronics and stops at the glass jewelry cabinet. She eyes what appears to be a brilliant emerald pendant propped on a gold setting and pictures it around the slender neck of her mother: the same mother that had spilled the wine on her jacket just days ago. She considers purchasing it with the money she has put aside for school and then saving the pendant all the way up until Mother's Day, when she would thank her mother for all that she had sacrificed for her. But just then, the clerk strolls over to her and asks her if she needs any help. Yes, she replies, as she unclasps her fingers and reveals a silver pocket watch, warm from the long while it spent in the safety of her fist. I'd like to sell this, she tells him straight. He swallows, glances down at the watch, looks back at her, and tells her the money she'll receive. The girl is disappointed and fidgets uncomfortably. Is that all? Yes. Never mind then, she tells him as she repositions the watch in her palm and closes her fingers hard. She opens the door and closes it calmly behind her. It was a stupid idea, she reflects. No, I am telling her, it wasn't. It was a warmhearted gesture that your family would have appreciated no matter the outcome. I hug her close to me as a tear rolls off her cheek and onto mine.

Marge got home from the office at six.

"You changed the combination again," I said as I felt her skirt brush past me.

"What did you expect?" I didn't turn around to follow her to the front door, but instead decided to stay there on the steps until she noticed me. I heard the door slam and soon realized I was on the wrong side of it. I waited for a while, but the cold was eating away at me. I gave up and banged on the door until Marge relented and let me in.

"You didn't notice me just sitting out there?"

"I think you're old enough to pay attention, don't you agree?" Her eyebrows formed even deeper folds in her forehead but relaxed as she picked up the mail and went upstairs. Once again, I stayed still, listening to the two-for-one Payless loafers making their way up two flights of stairs and coming to rest when Marge reached her office, the one place she could be sure she would never find me.

Later, Marge kindly notified me that she was going out. "I trust you can manage your own meal," she said.

"Yes," I said, not daring to annoy her by looking her in the eye.

"Alright, good."

Once I heard the door slam, I checked my watch and lay back on the couch to listen to the brilliant hum of an empty house.

Wednesday afternoon after school let out, I headed over to bus stop number forty-three as usual, staring at the cement as a matter of habit. I never for a moment considered her not being there. But as I eased myself onto the swinging rubber seats, I observed unfamiliar mud-coated sneakers instead of the clean leather boots I was accustomed to. As my gaze drifted upward, the unthinkable became clear. She wasn't there. It was a weekday at 3 p.m. and she was not there! In her place was a sorry-looking stranger with hard eyes and hard cheeks, a stranger who would never provide the brief smile I relied on. I wondered if she was late, but then again she had never been late for piano (she holds piano books on Wednesdays). Could she be sick? Not very likely, her mother gives her vitamins every morning. Is she visiting someone? But whom would she want to visit in the middle of the school week? Maybe she just forgot her music books and had to go back home to get them. That might happen. That's what had happened, so I decided to wait a little while just to make sure she found her music books OK. But there he was looking at me. His eyes cut directly into mine, and once they took hold they didn't let go. The street was gray, and silent, and empty. I was all alone with his sneering lips and bulging muscles, and I just knew he knew I was nervous. My mother had told me to never appear nervous in the presence of a possibly dangerous stranger. He shifted his weight on the seat. Now there were only centimeters left between his knee and mine. His gaze wasn't fixed on me, but I could tell he was watching me. He didn't need to look at me to see how scared I was, how insecure I felt when my one constant wasn't there to protect me. I got up suddenly, too suddenly. I should have gotten up slowly, but my heart was beating like insect wings and my legs could decide quicker than I could. I started walking away toward home, getting faster and faster every step. My feet were tempted to leave the ground, but I couldn't run. I knew he would still be watching me.

The next few days I didn't bother going back; I knew she wouldn't be there. Maybe I wouldn't have gone back at all if it had not been for my mother's business meeting. On Monday morning she announced that some of her coworkers were coming over that night to discuss their new deal with Viacom. And don't think that I wouldn't choose any activity other than witnessing Marge and five other black-suited weasels with paralyzed smiles make the windows vibrate with their "ingenious ideas." And it's not like I had rock climbing class or painting lessons or any friends to visit, so I didn't have any choice but to go to the bus stop. And besides, I had to know for sure if she had vanished or not. I heard yelling, angry, raspy yelling that made me yearn for Mozart. The reverberations off the sidewalk gradually inched closer until I saw one of the culprits. She had long hair that had been plastered straight and legs that appeared far too plentiful for the jeans that held them. On top she wore a jacket, puffy like down. It was exactly like the girl's, except black instead of cream. Despite her youthful clothing, I could tell even from far away that she was well over thirty. I heard her shout some sort of brutish insult to the other one, who was just rounding the corner. They slowly came closer to the bus stop until I could finally hear their conversation.

"Where in hell would you go?" the older one spat, turning toward the other one and blocking her path.

"I don't know, and, you know what, I don't really care as long as you're not there to push me around anymore." This one was much thinner and wore a white version of the jacket that the older one wore. Why was she carrying a suitcase? I looked down at my feet. I didn't want to look at them, but all of a sudden the young one dropped her suitcase and shoved the old one hard on the chest. She stepped back clumsily.

"You don't have any money!" the old one shouted, frustrated and bewildered. But it was already too late. The girl with the suitcase was already tearing down the street. Out of politeness, or maybe fear, I hadn't yet looked at their faces. But it didn't matter at all because I discovered her anyway. The one with the suitcase had nearly turned the corner, and I could see that on her puffy white jacket was a big, ugly splotch, the exact color of red wine.

[*From Dave Eggers's writing class. The assignment was to write a "cover story"—a story using the themes and basic architecture of a classic story. The hope is that students can learn about story structure—what makes a story work—by walking in the footsteps of masters. The following story was based on Edgar Allen Poe's "The Tell-Tale Heart."*]

The Mountain Patch-Nose Snake

by JAKE WATTERS

Age 16, Lowell High School

Yeah, I was nervous. I was totally nervous. Pretty nervous, really nervous. But when I decided upon it there was nothing to be nervous about. But I still felt so bad. I didn't want to steal it, but it just happened. The idea didn't even cross my mind. But still it happened.

Why would I even want to steal from him? I loved that store and I loved those sandwiches. I was a regular. I had gone to that store every day for a year and bought the same sandwich. Every day I walked through the door, an electronic beep sounded and he greeted me with a "how's it going today boss man?" and asked me if I wanted the usual. The usual was a turkey sandwich with avocado and canned jalapenos, but no mayo. I hated mayonnaise, still do. It's awful. It's like eating fat sucked out of someone, put into a jar and then onto your sandwich. Every day I walked down the aisles of shelves stocked with canned anchovies, boxes of crackers and bleach, to the back, where they kept the sodas. Every day I contemplated my choices. I decided which drink would go well with my sandwich that day. I bought my drink and my sandwich and left the store.

But last week it happened a bit differently. I walked in like it was any other day and I ordered the usual. I walked down the aisle of bleach and anchovies and I thought long and hard about what I would get to drink.

"Do I want an iced tea to refresh me in this warm weather?" I thought to myself. "I want to get a Yoohoo but it makes my mouth all mucusy. It's also a bit too filling with the sandwich. But then again, so are half the drinks in this fridge. I could get one of those energy drinks, but they taste like cough syrup. Or I could get cough syrup. Or maple syrup. The choices are endless."

I decided to get a Yoohoo and I pulled one out of the fridge. By the time I got back to the front of the store my sandwich was toasting in the oven. Toasting is the most crucial part of a good sandwich—besides the bread and the other things in the sandwich. So it's really more of a luxury than a must-have.

So that day last week, I decided to break routine. I decided I wanted a candy bar. I walked past the front counter and I grabbed a Skor bar and stuck it into my pocket, with the intent of paying for it later. I took a swig from my bottle of artificial chocolate drink, and began walking toward the counter. The wrapper from the candy bar crinkled in my pocket with every other step I took. It sounded like a cross between static, a maraca and crumpled-up piece of paper. I wondered what the noise was and realized it was the candy bar inside my pocket. My sandwich was done. I paid for it and the drink at the counter. It cost $6.55 and I dumped the change I got back into the tip-jar next to the register. I left the shop and walked back home.

That crinkling noise accompanied me on my journey home. I reached into my pocket to get my keys. Instead of my keys I found a rectangular cubish thing wrapped in plastic. I took it out of out pocket and looked at a Skor bar in my hand. "Why am I holding a candy bar?" I thought to myself. "Where could this have come from?" Then it hit me like a sack of heavyweight boxers, each wielding a sack of featherweight boxers: I had just stolen from the liquor store. I had stolen a candy bar from the liquor store. I didn't like the idea but it was true.

"Would he notice the missing candy bar? It's only a candy bar," I thought to myself. "Would he suspect *me* if he did notice? He wouldn't suspect ME; I go there all the time. Or would he? He does call me 'boss man.' But he calls everyone who goes in there more than twice 'boss man.' I've seen people steal from there before and he never caught them. They didn't try and return the things they stole, but still he didn't catch them. How would I even go about returning the candy bar? How would I tell him I accidentally stole a candy bar? Would he think less of me if I told him? If I told him would he purposely make a worse sandwich the next time? Is that possible? It's possible, all he does is put Italian dressing on it. But it's still good. I bet there's some way he could make a bad sandwich. I could pretend it didn't happen. I could just discreetly put it back in the tray tomorrow when I go there for lunch. Yes. That's it. That IS it!"

I decided I would just put it back in the box and pretend it didn't happen. The wrapper crinkled when I opened my hand. Anyway, pretty soon I looked down at my hand and saw what appeared to be the empty wrapper of the candy bar. Had I eaten it? I had.

I had no other choice. I needed to pretend I had not eaten/stolen the candy bar. I was confident that I could pull it off. He could not have known what I had done. I was so confident that I put the receipt and the wrapper in the pocket of my pants the next day when I went back, just to prove that I was untouchable, like Sean Connery, in that movie, except I won't get mowed down in a hail of gunfire. I would simply walk in, pay for my sandwich and drink, tip him and leave.

I went to the liquor/sandwich market the next day. I walked through the front door. I heard the same electronic beep and was greeted the same way I had always been. I ordered the usual and looked above the ovens that the sandwich guy uses to toast the sandwiches. But now all the sandwiches on the menu were 25 cents more expensive. Was the candy bar I stole the reason for this?

It couldn't be, right? How could a one-dollar candy bar missing result in a 25 cent increase in sandwich prices?

I heard something that sounded like a cross between static, a maraca and crumpled-up piece of paper. "The raise in prices must have been from that candy bar I stole," I thought to myself. I looked to see what was creating the noise but could not find a source.

"What's up with the prices?" I inquired.

"Meat—up," the sandwich man replied, his words drowned out by the crinkling. "—had—rices for—ears, —it's time to—ange—em."

"What now?" I asked.

But the crinkling became louder and louder. I felt like I had to scream to drown out the crinkle. I pretended I could hear him and I tried to make conversation. This was around the time that some hiker got stuck under a boulder and sawed off his arm to escape. It was all over the news. I tried to hide my horrified reaction to the crinkling for a while. I joked that cutting one's arm off with a pocketknife isn't that bad as long as you see the great outdoors. I paced back and forth in front of the sneeze-guarded table that held all the sandwich parts. I spoke louder and louder to get rid of the crinkling in my ear. No matter how loud I spoke or how hard I stomped my foot into the ground as I paced the crinkling got louder. I played with my keys in my pocket in an attempt to silence the noise with a soft jingle. I knew that he knew what I had done. The crinkling could only come from the wrapper in my pocket. And he knew I was horrified by the noise. He could hear the crinkling in my pocket. He knew I had stolen a candy bar but pretended he didn't. He talked normally and rang up my sandwich as he usually did but didn't accuse me, as if mocking me. I had to scream; it was the only way it would end. The crinkling got louder, so loud that every crinkle sounded like a mountain being broken in half.

"Villain!" I screamed at the man across the counter. "Hide it no more! I admit it! I stole the candy bar! In my pocket is the wrapper and the receipt from which that sweet was absent! It is the crinkling of that hideous wrapper!"

[From Dave Eggers's writing class. The assignment was to write a "cover story"—a story using the themes and basic architecture of a classic story. The hope is that students can learn about story structure—what makes a story work—by walking in the footsteps of masters. The following story was based on Carson McCullers's "Mme. Zilensky and the King of Finland."]

Mme. Bruchard and the Tomato Trees

by AMELIA ROSENMAN

Age 17, *Lick-Wilmerding High School*

When I met Mme. Bruchard, she was clearly Vietnamese, though she had sounded French enough on the phone. Not that I mind particularly either way. I'm all for exotic, and believe me, she looked straight off a coconut plantation when she showed up smiling wide and saying she was my new tenant—she and the four little ones who trailed behind her. I could never keep the girls' names in my head, so I got to calling them Left, Right, Up, and Down, since that's where each one would look when you talked at her. Plus I figured it would help them learn some useful English.

The first time I paid them a neighborly visit, Mme. Bruchard was in a sweat. I figured that was fairly expectable from a dance teacher, and I waited as she dried her face off with a curtain and gave rapid instructions to the girls in French. It may as well have been: "Hurry hurry hurry! Look shifty-eyed and fidget! The handsome landlord is here! I am sweating!"

After cooling off, she slumped at the kitchen table next to me and offered, "Would you like, eat something? I make new brioche."

"Oh no, don't trouble yourself," I said. "Please. I'll just have a glass of water."

"No no no, I already make new brioche," she said, and hurried into the kitchen. She returned with a plate of alternately flat and puffy objects.

"Thank you," I said, taking one from the plate. It was a tough, salty, determined kind of brioche. "Delicious," I murmured.

"I was five-star cook in Paris. Many times our bakery in papers!" she glowed.

"I can imagine," I said, though I could not. Mme. Bruchard sprinted back into the kitchen, returning this time with Coke and lemon.

"You like this? Lemon?" she asked. I nodded. "I once worked in a lemon orchard. I still smell them times," she said.

"How do you say lemon in French?" I asked, for no good reason.

"Fraise."

"Fraise," I repeated, and I caught her smirking at me. I figured the way I rolled my "r" amused her.

After a few weeks, I began to notice certain things about Mme. Bruchard. First of all, she never slept. No matter what hour I leaned over my balcony to peer through her window, the light was on in her kitchen. I figured she either received choreographic inspiration by night, or else practiced a dangerously oriental moon vigilance.

One morning, I caught her bright lip-sticked and alert as ever, pushing the girls out the door. I asked her what she had been up to the night before.

"Oh, dreams!" she beamed. "Dreams about my mother trying to sing the Marseillaise!"

"Funny," I said, "that you sleep with the light on and all."

Mme. Bruchard swung her head dramatically toward her left shoulder. "We are gone!" she announced, and they left.

Next I noticed that Mme. Bruchard did not demonstrate natural mothering instincts. She kept her flat rugless, lampshade-less, and basically free of decoration, aside from a colorful Ivory Soap advertisement taped crudely above the bathroom sink in place of a mirror, and presumably, of real soap. She rarely showed affection to Down, Up, Left, and Right, though she sometimes tugged their dresses in one direction or another in a violent straightening effort that left each girl with red chafing stripes on her shoulders. Once, when the littlest ran to her, sucking a thumb that was obviously bleeding, Mme. Bruchard dismissed her without looking up: "Oh, no, child—it was a red pen."

The third thing I noticed was that Mme. Bruchard clung, with an unhealthy and unexplained fervency, to a small brown notebook that looked quite worn. I never once saw her without it, and I never once saw her open, read, or write in it. I did see her once, however, sitting on the steps to the apartment as she waited for the girls, rocking the notebook between her arms, singing softly.

One evening in October, Mme. Bruchard burst breathless into my apartment.

"I left my baby at the dentist's!" she cried.

"Oh no! Let's hurry, I'll drive you, quick—" I grabbed my keys and started for the door.

"No," she said. "It's been too long. She's probably grown up." Mme. Bruchard's eyes were growing large.

"How long has it been?" I asked, puzzled.

"Seven years."

"Seven *years*?"

"Why did I leave her with him? She had such pretty nose and face. And she was my child!" She was sobbing now.

"Whoa there. Start from the beginning," I said.

"My l-last child, I left her with her father."

"And her father was a dentist?"

"Yes." For a minute we were both silent.

"Well, I'm—I'm sure he's taking good care of her," I offered. "What did the father of the other girls do?" I asked, trying to take her mind somewhere else.

"How do they say? Butcher, baker, candlestick maker. And, a poet."

"Ha ha! Well, huh. I'm sure, well I'm sure the other one will have, well, pretty teeth."

"Yes. I am certain." Mme. Bruchard's face was blank and her breathing slowed. She turned and left without closing the door.

Learning of the girls' multiple fathers confused me, since they all looked alike and looked nothing like Mme. Bruchard. Learning of a fifth forgotten child, however, surprised me less, as Mme. Bruchard was constantly misplacing her shoes, her coat, and, periodically, the meal she was preparing for dinner.

As the days began trimming themselves for winter, Mme. Bruchard continued to bustle her way from home to work and work to home. The girls wrapped their mouths around new English words with that curious way of foreigners, who look like they are tasting a new and unwieldy fruit with each syllable. I spent my time as usual, penning petty poetry by day and ripping it up by night. One evening, I was puzzling over a line overburdened with metaphor when I suddenly remembered something strange Mme. Bruchard had said earlier in the day.

I had been helping her unload some heavy file cabinets from her car, when she turned to me and laughed.

"Your fingers are so red in the cold! They remind me of the tomatoes I used to pick. Ah, the way our backs would ache from the climbing and climbing, all the little red tomatoes and the farthest branches."

I didn't think much of it at the time, preoccupied as I was with transporting the steel containers up the stairs. But later in the night, I stood up from my poem and beamed with my sudden revelation. Mme. Bruchard was an unequivocal, unapologetic, pathological liar. Every word she had uttered from the very first phone conversation had been a casually constructed, fantastical, frivolous untruth. She had never been a famous baker. That was clear enough from the questionable edibility of her kitchen experiments. She didn't sleep at night, let alone dream. Instead she spent her nights beneath her glowing light, concocting the next lies she would like to believe, and writing them down in the mysterious notebook she carried around. She didn't leave her fifth daughter with a dentist; she didn't have a fifth daughter. She merely invented this last abandoned child so that she could trust someone, even an imaginary kid, to carry her name into the future more gloriously than she or any of her real daughters would. She had lied about them, too. All her children were of the same mahogany-colored father whom she would rather replace with four stand-ins than remember in truth. She had never picked lemons—her hands were not the stained and weathered tools of a fruit-picker, and she had just proved to me that she had certainly never picked tomatoes. I was furious. I was ecstatic.

I skated down the stairs to knock on her apartment door. She opened it a gap and smiled her curry-sweet smile out at me. "Yes?"

"Mme Bruchard!" I could hardly contain myself. "Mme. Bruchard! You said this morning that you used to pick tomatoes on trees?"

"Yes of course, in the time between the baker and the—"

"But Mme. Bruchard. Tomatoes don't grow on trees! You've made it up, Mme. Bruchard. It's not possible. It's not scientifically possible!"

"They were warm and sweet, even with the traces of dirt."

"Mme Bruchard—"

"I used to lean down and feed them to the girls. They would pop them in their mouths like candy. Just like can—"

"TOMATOES DON'T GROW ON TREES!" I shouted.

She raised her voice triumphantly: "When they got too ripe they would drop and splatter on the grass, and—"

"Mme. Bruchard, you are lying to me," I whispered.

She looked up sharply, her head vibrating uncontrollably. She stared at me for a few seconds, then closed her eyes and shook her head slowly, moaning to herself in low tones. Her bright face and innocent voice had turned aged and shuddering. In her tuneless drone I could hear the lives she had built up for herself flattened into one unwavering note. I felt suddenly like a rapist. I had ruthlessly stripped her of the fictional skins in which she wrapped herself. Now she stood before me naked and freezing. I bit my lip and cried a little, silently. After a few minutes, she stopped her moaning and looked up slowly like a moon afraid to rise.

"Oh Mme. Bruchard," I begged, trembling with regret, reaching out for her hand, "How I wish I could taste tomatoes like those."

[This story is from Dave Eggers's writing class. The assignment here was fairly loose. The class was working on revealing character and developing tension through dialogue. Ideally, the words spoken would ring true, but would say more than they appeared to say.]

A Case of the Gimme Gimmes

by KERRY TIEDEMAN

Age 16, Burlingame High School

A foul scent lurks in my history classroom. I tell myself to breathe, that the day is almost over. (Isn't it?) I stretch my legs out under the desk, leaning my weight against the cold chair. I kick Igor, the mullet head in front of me. He doesn't say anything, but quickly moves his feet away from mine. I laugh to myself. I don't understand how some boys can be intimidated by a foot touching theirs.

Ms. Costa stops the quiz. "Is anyone hot? They want to boil us in here!" She walks briskly over to the windows in her two-inch high heels, her fat butt hanging out.

"But I'm cold!" Dinah yells out, not realizing the volume of her voice. It's funny how someone with an IQ of 150 can't function socially.

Ms. Costa gives her a nasty look, failing to hide her hatred for Dinah. Dinah doesn't catch on to the fact that Ms. Costa doesn't like being corrected all the time. "Move to the other side, away from the windows," she says to Dinah.

Dinah agrees too readily, sliding into a seat next to the love of her life, Mullethead, and kitty corner to mine. I run my pen along Mullethead's shoulders. He squirms, faking a natural reaction. It always makes me smile.

"I like it over here," Dinah squawks.

She's the type of girl my dad would call *beaker*. My classmates whisper to each other, berating the poor girl. The truth is I like Dinah. I like her abrasive personality and bold humor. She's not afraid. She smiles in Mullethead's direction, revealing chocolate on her teeth. I just shake my head while Mullethead and I grade each other's quizzes. I start drawing hearts on his, coloring them with yellow highlighter. I think about the time when these hearts were more than silly decorations. But like every boy in my life, Mullethead ceased to interest me. You could call it wanting what you can't have, you could call it loving the chase. Heck, you could call it whatever you wanted to. I didn't care. It was plain and simple. The same thing has happened with Penis Nose and Gap Tooth. I haven't cut back on my flirting, and I don't think I will anytime soon. I do feel bad about Mullethead, but I like the perfect scores I have been getting on my quizzes lately.

The bell rings loudly in my ear. I heave the overwhelming backpack onto my bad shoulder and immediately make a run for the doorway. I need to breathe.

I enter sixth period two minutes later. From the left corner of the room I hear a deep voice call out, "Good afternoon Kerry!" I flash a smile in Tyson's direction. He's the only one in chem. class right now. Davin and Kristy come in a second after me. Davin crashes into his seat next to mine. I immediately take the opportunity to tease him about the new girl in his life.

"So Davin how's the latest girl? I saw you guys at the talent show."

Davin gives me a confused look. This is the only subject that he really doesn't say much about. It's a good way to shut him up.

"Is she cute?"

"What do *you* think?" Davin asks, reminding me that the chauvinistic jerk he was would never be caught dead with a less-than-par girl.

I ignore his comment. "Ya know, I think you should just ask her to hang out, forget all that Will-you-be-my-girlfriend crap." Tyson nods his head. Kristy joins in our conversation.

"Yeah, it always seems you ask one girl out, then you get dumped within two days. Maybe you're doing something wrong."

Davin shoots her a dirty look. He takes out his camera phone, and shows us a picture of a girl, and smiles, thinking it will prove that he does have a decent chance with her. In the picture she's crossing her eyes and sticking out her tongue.

"I so would hit that!" Kristy laughs.

"It's a bad picture!" Davin insists. I look at Davin and think of how quickly I shot him down when he asked me out. These days he has trouble looking at me.

Ms. Marcan interrupts my thought, yelling from the front of the room, "Get your asses to the lab stations!" Our little corner group fails to realize that class has begun. I groan, thinking of how far the two-foot walk is to the lab stations. We all get up and trudge to the tables. Kristy and I waste ten minutes laughing at Tyson struggling to fit his huge hands into the latex gloves. Tyson is no small guy. I run my hands along his, trying to help him out. He just blunders more, attempting to keep his composure. After his third attempt, Ms. Marcan wanders over.

"What the hell is taking you so long?" she asks.

"Tyson is having problems with the gloves. His hands are too big," I tell her.

"So why doesn't someone with smaller hands do it?" She looks at Kristy and me.

"I can't take the smell of those things," Kristy answers. Ms. Marcan looks her up and down, viewing the rather strange outfit Kristy has on today, losing concentration on the lab.

"Denim jacket, plaid dress, khaki zippered pants, and black shoes with red laces?"

"She's making a fashion statement," I say. Kristy, Ms. Marcan, and I look over Ms. Marcan's outfit.

"Yeah my skort is really fashionable," she says sarcastically. "I wear this 'cause I know if I wore a real skirt my fat cow thighs would rub together."

"That would be disastrous," Kristy smiles.

I laugh hysterically.

"Do whatever you want for the last one and half minutes," Ms. Marcan yells to the classroom. Just as she finishes, the bell rings. I fumble around with my books while the boys are leaving. Kristy walks past me, but turns, "Do you like even one of them?" she says, "Cause it's messed up and you know it."

She doesn't wait for a response. I frown at her harsh tone, but before I can give it a second thought, my cell phone rings. Penis Nose is on the other line. I know I shouldn't, but it's just a little conversation right? Kristy isn't always right. I click answer, and walk out the door.

[This story is from Dave Eggers's writing class. The assignment here was fairly loose. The class was working on revealing character and developing tension through dialogue. Ideally, the words spoken would ring true, but would say more than they appeared to say.]

And They Both Suspect That Somehow This Is All Completely Irrelevant

by RACHEL BOLTEN

Age 16, Castilleja School

Here is inevitability, here is conversation. These are the words which he says. Here is what she replies. Mathematically, Matt takes up approximately 78 percent of the conversation. She, called Lea for short, takes up another 9 percent. The rest we leave to awkward silences.

Pausing in the hall between third and fourth period, Matt achieves that inevitability, that conversation.

"Hello," he says.

And she replies:

"Hello."

Matt wants to talk about their plans; their most magniminicious megarifical plans for the summer, each drawn up with unparalleled attention to detail during Friday morning study period.

One of these plans involves driving around in Matt's old-new '92 Jetta, up and down the sprinkler-dotted asphalt hallways of suburbia searching for lemonade stands. They will buy a glass from each stand they find—with a single mix tape on repeat for weeks at a time—bringing love, truth, and beauty with them everywhere they go, messengers of ridiculously cheesy bohemian ideals ripped off from that *Moulin Rouge* movie. They will share stuff, all and any important stuff because that is what they will do and then they will contemplate the relativity of importance.

"So. How're you? I mean, since we last talked, what's up?," asks Matt.

Lea replies:

"Ummnothing. Fine. Yourself?"

"Pretty much the same as always. You know, yeah. Meh."

"So. Matt."

(silence.)

(silence.)

Next, before moving to take over the world in a pet-friendly international dictatorship, they will descend upon the café downtown, next to that favorite bookstore, stereo in hand. The intricate plan involves that song, that one song from *Singin' in the Rain* where Gene Kelly and the girl and that other really funny guy who died, yeah, Donald O'Connor, do that dance thing. They will play the music and count off the beats and begin to dance, musical-style, between the tables and chairs. Soon, everyone else, the rest of the people at the café, will get up and start dancing too, and it will be just like the movies because everyone will want to dance with them and they will take over the El Camino, dancing and singing in a giant formation and people will want to get out of their cars and dance too and they will be on the 10 o'clock news and this will be like world-domination but better and everyone will want to join their incredible parade of joy and terror and—oh. my. God.—and that girl that Matt's had a crush on since seventh grade might be there and—

Oh man this is going to be great. This summer, these plans for the summer between sophomore and junior year are great. This summer is going to be sosogreat.

"So, there's this thing this weekend…," says Matt, hopefully.
"Can't."
"Why?"
"Busy."
"Right. Right. Ok, see you later? I mean, I'm guessing, yeah. Maybe something next weekend? See you study period."
"We aren't in that together anymore. I gotta go."
"Bye."
"Bye." Lea turns away.
"Best friends, right?"
"Matt…"
"Right?"
"*(sigh)* Best friends."

Lea is short for something but no one really remembers what, even her parents. She has no interest in discussing these "magniminicious megarifical" plans with Matt. Lea will go to Paris in July with her family, where she will not drink lemonade out of colorful plastic cups on the sidewalk and where she will not break out into musical dance routines in the middle of the Champs-Elysées. (Although there are a few choice songs that would be perfect for such an occasion.)

No, Lea does not want to talk about those plans, she has nothing to say on the subject.

She instead wants to say:

Matt. I know we were friends. I know we were good friends. I know we were best friends. I know you still think we are I know we aren't anymore. Matt. We aren't in study period together anymore. Matt. You made up all those stupid plans. Matt. This tension is horrible, this tension sucks. Screw it, Matt, it's no longer subtle. Matt. We are not friends anymore; we have not been friends for a while now. Matt. You need to stop this, stop this, stop this, Matt. Just stop talking to me because this tension, this pressure to converse is standing over me like something big and scary and AHHH! and I don't want to stand in its shadow any more and Matt. Can't we just *move on*? The passing of time is inevitable, Matt, you can't stop change. Crap, that's trite. I'm getting all teary-eyed, now. Here's the real shocker, too, Matt. Next year is not junior year, Matt. That summer, where we could've done everything you say and where I actually would've wanted to share all that important stuff with you, that summer was two years ago. Don't forget that. Why are you confused? That summer was two years ago and next fall we're going off to college. And screw you, Matt, screw you because I want to still be best friends but that's not gonna happen and I know I'll never see you again because I don't want to but I wish you all the best all the same next year (wherever it is you're going), all the best all the same. But this was always inevitable.

Say something, Matt! *(Awkward silence number 2. Blah blah blah blah blah. Say something, Matt. You knew this was coming. Dammit. Number 3.)*

Then one day Matt receives it. It is a postcard. Getting mail is so exciting. Fantastic. Excitement is always welcome, here, where Matt has spent June and the first two weeks of July lying on his stomach in the backyard. Grass looks interesting, close up. From above, grass appears a single green mass but eye to eye each blade stares back. Emerald foreground, to muted background. Matt has noted this many times, shifting the focus of his eyes. Once, earlier in June, his neighbor Sam called and asked him if he wanted to go down to Great America, just to hang out. Matt said no, said he had plans, and in the afternoon he took a walk down the street. Two blocks down, some kids were selling lemonade. It was salty. A disappointment. The phone hasn't rang for Matt since then. A failure.

Matt sets the postcard down on the kitchen counter.

The back says (It is lacking a "salutation."):

Paris is nice. Yesterday, I went to the Eiffel Tower. It was cool. Having a great time. Gotta go.

Lea

Front: a picture of the Eiffel Tower. Granted, Lea is not in the picture. (segue into metaphor.)

No, no. Lea is no longer a part of the picture, no longer a part of his life. (WHAM! Metaphor.) There is a moment of realization, simultaneously followed by denial, which Matt experiences at this point.

Matt talks to/with himself, saying:

"No. No. Who're you kidding?"

"We *are* friends."

"No. Matt. No."

"YES WE ARE!"

"You're pathetic."

"*SO*? So are you."

Matt draws himself to the sidelines of his mind for a pep-talk. Here are internal dialogues, continuous conversation. This is not a new thought, no. Not at all. Before, it could be ignored, overruled. Good triumphing over evil, KABLAM. Which is not to say that this was an evil thing. The terms are simply used figuratively. But usually, Matt could convince himself that he was only confused, that she was still his friend. He could make little excuses for himself, for her. She didn't call him because she had lost her cell phone. She couldn't do anything on the weekends because she was too busy. She didn't want to talk to him right then because she had to get to class. She couldn't go out to lunch because she had already eaten and she was supposed to do something with her family.

Excuse A, excuse B. She didn't write him a postcard because her trip was just *jam-packed* wait no. *Wait. No.* She did send a postcard. And he had thought that the fact that she had sent it was fantastic!

But the insignificance of that postcard is unbearable. What had he been expecting? A long long *letter*, at least? A plane, flying high in the sky over San Francisco at a Giants game with a banner trailing behind proclaiming their friendship? Oh, this is really not so fantastic as before! This is a time for self-pity and for mint-chip ice cream!

Matt counts the words. There are twenty. This is insignificant, an insignificant number in comparison to the flow of many words streaming through his mind, proclaiming instead of their friendship a *loss* undying.

Silence. Then, silently. Matt tacks the postcard onto the bulletin board at his desk to remind him not to try again.

[*This story is from an assignment in Dave Eggers's writing class. The students were asked to read Jamaica Kincaid's story "Girl" and adapt that story's use of the imperative voice as a way to reveal context and characters.*]

Chrysanthemums

by CHELSEA DAVIS

Age 15, Crystal Springs Uplands School

Go out and get something, it's his birthday tomorrow; get some flowers, I don't know… Because I'm tired, do you know what kind of a crappy day I've had? And now this. How am I supposed to—yeah, fine, roses. No, wait a second, roses would be obscene… buy some chrysanthemums. Get the red kind. They are not for Christmas, why would you say that? No, they're fine, get the chrysanthemums! Shut up! Violets, fine, if you're so goddamn sure that violets are right. You always have to be right. Could you turn that thing off for just one second? Turn it off! Just… listen. God, my back hurts. Everything hurts. No, it doesn't matter. Forget it. I said it doesn't matter! Just go get the violets! Go to that place on 5th, Dolores's, or whatever. I don't care, just… look… Oh, Jesus, don't start this now, it's his birthday tomorrow— it would have been his birthday tomorrow. Just get the violets, those soft dark purple flowers. We'll bring them there tomorrow. Oh God, look, I'm sorry, please don't cry. Crap, don't cry. I thought… I thought we were over… just get the violets, please, just get the goddamn violets.

[*This story is from an assignment in Dave Eggers's writing class. The students were asked to read Jamaica Kincaid's story "Girl" and adapt that story's use of the imperative voice as a way to reveal context and characters.*]

Untitled

by AMELIA ROSENMAN

Age 17, Lick-Wilmerding High School

Double latte./ No, no milk./ Please, low fat./ To go./ Actually can I get it in two cups?/ Hot chocolate, one inch of foam, extra hot./ How much?/ What did you say? Yes, it's raining outside./ A bran muffin and an Evian, thanks./ Can I get a shot of cinnamon in that?/ A spoon, please./ Sorry?/ What kind of accent is that?/ Mocha, small./ Mocha, large./ Decaf coffee, leave room for milk./ Do you have a restroom?/ What's that? Yes, it's still raining. Can't you see? It's shooting at us./ Steamed milk./ No, it's a silver dollar./ A hot chai, please. And what's that one there? Okay, I'll take one of those in a bag for the bus, thank you./ Fruit smoothie, please, yes, ice./ What kind of accent is that?/ Did you just crush that woman's ice with your bare hands?/ Why are you erasing the menu?/ Do you have two-percent milk?/ Do you have cider?/ What kind of a place has no cider?/ What kind of accent is—/ Are you sure there's no coffee?/ I'd like to use the—/ You spilled it all over the—/ Stop! That's my straw! You're blowing bubbles through my straw!/ What kind of place is—/ No, it's stopped raining. Yes, it's perfectly clear./ Where are you running to? What do we owe you?

[This story is from an assignment in Dave Eggers's writing class. The students were asked to read Jamaica Kincaid's story "Girl" and adapt that story's use of the imperative voice as a way to reveal context and characters.]

Insert Title Here
(A Weird Rant Thing)

by Elizabeth Neveu

Age 16, UC Berkeley

Be clever. Be decisive. Speak up. Speak out. Make an impact. Be funny. Be outgoing. Exercise a large vocabulary. No swearing. *(Sarcasm is the lowest form of wit?)* No stuttering. Be weary of spoonerisms. *(I hope I used that word right— err, correctly.)* Write something original. Avoid whiny teen-angst crap. Be conscious of your spelling. *(Ya know what's a weird word? Conscience. And as much as I—ahem—dislike Helen Hunt, it is kinda funny that it's spelled con.science. Hey, you never finished watching* As Good As It Gets, *did you?)* FOCUS! Plot... plot... theme... find a theme, and stick to it. You have a time limit, remember? Listen to your teachers. Stop spacing out. Drink less coffee. Drink more coffee. Stop backspacing! Continue writing even if it's dumb... Umm... I don't like popcorn or Russell Crowe. Yeah. That was dumb. Note to self: write more frequently. Write write write. The English language is a beautiful thing. German is cooler though. I mean really! "Globe" in German is "Erdball." Earth. Ball. Earthball. Way cooler than English... Whoa, I don't even have half a page yet. You do realize you don't even have half a page yet, don't you? Think think. Think. Helen Keller was a socialist; did you know that? FOCUS! Think of something witty. Always have deep characters. Never use the word deep to describe something. Ever. You'll sound like some idiot in front of an abstract painting who has no idea what to say. So, uh, have, *multifaceted* characters. Crap! Get back on track. Did I have a track? You idiot, you don't even have a track? Aw man… you shouldn't have stayed up so late. Your brain would be working more *efficiently* (praise spell check) if you had slept. And had more than coffee and a smoothie today. Take care of your body. Remember to eat. If you get that far try eating *healthy*. And finish reading what you start. You've started some pinchingly good books. Why did I type pinchingly? Hmm, odd word. But, well, I mean, they are like a pinch. It's like the evil reality fairy is pinching you and snickering, "Are you letting this *inspire* you? Wait, wait, wait, hold on a second…" (fairy feigns stumbling backwards and falling on ass) "You don't actually think you could ever write something even *half* that good do you?" Yeah. That's all I ever do. Read but not write. Then I don't finish what I read. Or what I write, when I actually gather myself together enough *to* write. Hey wait, so, I read all the time— why can't I speed read? Or can I already but… don't… realize it? Nah, I don't speed-write. I *savor* the words, damn it. How many books and plays and things *are* you reading right now? Don't read so much fantasy! What are you hiding from—the world or something? Be more political. Watch the news and stuff. But, hey, Michael Moore made a point about the news being crappy. Bah! Excuses! Seriously though, read some newspapers. And dress smartly. You look weird. Weird is OK—don't you *dare* look "normal"—weird is *fine*. But look *smart*-weird. What the hell is smart-weird? I guess more of an outgoing-weird and less of just a weird-weird. Yeah. Definitely. Speak up. Don't be so damn shy. No one in the history of *every*thing got *any*where by being shy. Ever. *Ever*, ever. Why didn't you read your writing exercise thing in front of the class last week? 'Cause you can't read your handwriting? No! Because you're a mole! Go crawl somewhere and hide, you damn mole! Hmm, add dork to that, you just called yourself a mole. Well, hey, the handwriting excuse *coulda* worked. I mean, your handwriting is atrocious (again, thank god for spell check). Note to self: improve handwriting. Damn, I was supposed to tell a story thing wasn't eye? Oh my god, you just typed "eye" instead of "I." And then you typed that you typed it. Hey, no backspacing, though. Remember? Edit this crap later. *(Shouldn't this have a "natural arc?" Is there an arc in this? There's no arc in this. Damn it.)* How the hell am I going to edit this, it's mostly train of thought randomness. Who the hell writes like this? This is crap. Well, P.G. Wodehouse writes in a weird train-of-thought style, but that's absolutely hilarious. Jeeves + Wooster = awesome. Hey, you didn't finish reading that, did you? AHH! You're HOPELESS. OK, OK, where was I? Gotta. Find. Place. Gotta think of something. Write about a... wait. Crap. Something about a... something. A what? Man. This is kind of embarrassing... Ooo! You know what might be cool? Some short story thing about the life of a quarter and, ya know, it gets passed around and spent and—hmm—that could actually turn into something if you could actually write. At all. Well, as long as you write something. Anything. Bad writing can be revised. Nonexistent writing can't. Have an interesting plot. *Have* a plot. In absence of plot, imply some deeper meaning. Remember: "ocean" means forever and metaphors for loneliness and death come in abundance. Man, I can't stand crap like that. I consider myself open-minded. I do. But that super vague, abstract stuff that grabs the title "avant-garde" and hides behind it while waggling its tongue at you? Nonsensical bull that nobody understands, but, oh! It's not *about* having a theme or a plot, it's about *us*. Us the audience and how *we* feel, and how *we* are affected by a plotless, themeless, waste of time. Crap is OK. Go ahead and create crap. But realize that it is crap. Yup. I realize this is crap. But, hey, you wrote something, didn't you? And I'm sure if I look real hard I'll find some themes and things. Unconscious themes are probably all over the place. And, if not, you'll write more stuff. So yeah! Screw the fairy.

Just... make sure you have a good ending.

WORD PORTRAITURE

[In this workshop, taught by Micah Pilkington, we learned how to make masterpiece portraits using words instead of paint. We discussed the history of portraiture, the art of perspective, and a variety of styles ranging from Renaissance to abstract. The word-artists then set to work, capturing the essence of a live model in his or her very fancy costume. After completing these pieces, they created word portraits of people they knew, rocks, computer monitors, and, somewhat surprisingly, elves.]

Word Portaits

by RYAN LOUGHRAN, *Age 10*; ARNO ROSENFOLD, *Age 9*;
KATIE LOUGHRAN, *Age 9*; CHRIS DAVISON, *Age 7*;
RADFORD "AGENT NO-NAME" LEUNG, *Age 10*;
NIDALIA "NIKKI" NAZZAL, *Age 9*

They Are Wearing...

Cowboy hats, wigs, necklaces, earrings, sunglasses, crazy shoes, doctor stuff, dresses, crazy tights! Watches, rings, tutus, skirts, lip gloss, flowers, crazy hair. Ages: 113 and 4. Names: Winky Dinky and Pinky Stinky. They are friends.

—Katie

It Is Not a Boy

It is green, long, brown.
It is a little blue.
It has a name; its name is Chicio.
It likes pizza and ice cream.
It is a palm tree,
Not a boy!

—Ryan

Portrait of a Computer Monitor

Silver gray cords coming out
   like a waterfall
Seeing the inner self.
The top holding an overcast feeling
Like a fog bank over San Francisco.
An apple growing
Off it, slanting and falling to legs.
Holes leaking air.

—Arno

A Terrifying, Boneless Rock

Boneless, gray, hard, heavy, rough, moldy. It's not grass. It is not anything but a weird, cold, big, stinky, book-reading, writing, million-year-old rock that is terrifying and also hurt.

—Radford

The Elves

Elves are really short and funny. They have really long beards and they never shave. They are sometimes strict and mean. Elves have big eyes and sideburns, and they wear pointy hats and shoes. They eat only rocks and have bad teeth.

—Nidalia

Yamcha

He has pointed hair and even if he wanted it flat, it would stay pointy. (But he doesn't want it pointy.) A funny thing about him is that in Chinese, Yamcha means "drink tea."

—Chris

MAKING POEMS I:
RESPONDING TO POETIC VOICES

[This workshop, taught by Laurel Newby and Renata Ewing, studied poems by major poets in order to inspire our students' writing. There were many in-class writing exercises which included revising and shaping the poems we wrote during class. At the completion of this workshop, the students published a collection of their work entitled A Poem Is Worth a Thousand Pictures.*]*

Selections from
A Poem Is Worth a Thousand Pictures

My Social Life

by MARIEKE THOMAS

Age 13, Herbert Hoover Middle School

Susan, Ching-Ching, Lauren, Girl Scout
Cookies, selling, Safeway, shoplift samples,
Eating, houses, swapping, chores, mopping,
Cleaning, gleaming, crystal goblet, wine, drink,
Kitchen sink, faucet, runny nose, funny
Joke, laugh, take a bath after gym, run, sun,
hot, heat, water drink, can't think, science, math,
feel my wrath, sword, stone, throne of bone, can't
    atone, human sin,
can't fight, won't win, don't spin, stomach flip,
    human,
belly flop, dive, hop, jelly drop, sweet, eat,
angel cute, little sister, me, Tommy, feet blister,
skate, ski, woe is me, him, he, pizzeria,
shop, fall, sparrow call, Jacky with a "y" no "e,"
teachers, reachers, work, home, busy bee,
me.

Untitled

by Marieke Thomas

Age 13, Herbert Hoover Middle School

Last night the snow lay glittering
like diamonds
against your milk-white neck
so elegant, so swanlike,
and yet, would having a three-foot long
neck make one beautiful?
Your fingers were long and fragile
as they groped the lacy tablecloth.

Cat takes a look at the weather
and decides it is stormy, curls
up next to the heater instead
blocking the way so I couldn't
dry my hair, wet after a fresh shower
water streaming in turrets down my back
has anyone ever told you to imagine
an audience naked?

The sea at evening moves across the sand
lodged deeply in my ancient, dilapidated
    sneakers
which I wear for all purposes;
to the beach, at home, to my ballet class
surrounded by prim pink primadonnas
with their long hair pinned neatly back in
a bun and their starved legs.

Untitled

by RADFORD LEUNG

Age 10, Commodore Sloat Elementary School

Under the leaves the croaking frog
flies to the moon and blows the fire.
Away against purple ships I saw from
the bus that light blue rainbow as the
girl wanders about in the window of
doom. She wanted to say, "Now it's time to say
what you wanted to say," but doom sighed
instead. She steps into the dark and
gazes at the moon as coins fall from
the sky.

White

by CHLOE CHEN

Age 10, Wild Oaks School

White like the blank sheet of paper;
White like the paper cup;
White like that T-shirt;
White like the pretty rose.

People overlook this color,
This blank, empty color,
The color that cannot be made by mixing
    other colors;
The one and only…
            White.

Five Ways of Looking
a Gift Horse in the Mouth

by MARIEKE THOMAS

Age 13, Herbert Hoover Middle School

I.
At a birthday party—
cake, candles, and party favors
and a bad hostess.

II.
Christmas excitement,
people forget
it's the thought that counts.

III.
People expect,
don't realize,
giving gifts is optional.

IV.
I didn't remind people
my birthday was coming up.
They forgot.

V.
She told me
jokingly
I couldn't come without
A gift.

Untitled

by Luna Alba Argueta
Age 13, AP Giannini Middle School

She glances into the
Dark…
And takes a running leap.
But a cricket can be heard
Off in the unseen
Distance
… Lost
With but a cloud
To guide her through
The blind path she's created for
Herself…
Deeper into the tunnel
She roams…
Not seeing the
Crumbs
She left behind
When she turns to find
Her way
Back…

Untitled

by Tyler Kubota

Age 9, Clarendon Elementary School

I am watching a woman swim in my
swimming pool. She doesn't notice as I
come out, as her boyfriend comes out to
the pool and asks what is love like? As
I come out with a cell phone and a
stun gun. As the winter evening settles down.
I threaten to call the police but
they ignore me. One minute later the police
   come
but to the wrong house.

I'm a little bug that is stuck on a ladybug. I make
the ladybug look like it has spots. I also make
dinosaurs extinct. Let's see me stuck on a
ladybug! If there were no ladybugs we would
make the humans extinct.

The moon is full tonight. I locked my
door and got my gun. I heard a howl
and so I loaded my gun. I passed the time
reading. I heard another howl. I looked outside and saw a werewolf. I ran
to the other door. Another werewolf.
I was doomed.

Blue

by GRACE NEVEU

Age 12, Home-schooled

The color blue
The color of the sky
The color blue
I watch it as I lie
The color blue
The perfect thing to see
The color blue
The ideal thing to be
The color blue
Is just for me

Where to Find a Poem

by KATE MEHL

Age 8, St. Philip's School

China.
In my head.
In my bed.
In my Mom's room.
In a pool.
Up a tree trunk.
In the water beneath the slime.

Hill

by SIOBHÁN WILLING
Age 13, Home-schooled

A hill on a farm. No cows graze upon this hill.
Only a lone eagle soars above the green mound
Of dirt and grass.

Everyone who passes this hill remembers
Some small detail from their life
That they have been unknowingly longing to
    remember.

Evil

by SIOBHÁN WILLING
Age 13, Home-schooled

They say that money is the root of all evil.
I think that it's jazz.

HOW TO BRING DOWN THE HOUSE

[*In a workshop entitled "How to Bring Down the House," taught by Micah Pilkington, a group of eleven- to fourteen-year-olds conquered territory that frightens most adults: they wrote autobiographical stories, then performed them in front of an audience. After hours of furious writing and some help from the Story Monkey, the class staged a reading for family, friends, and pirate store patrons that ended in applause. Thankfully, there was no structural damage to 826 Valencia.*]

Stitch It Up

by BETH LEVIN

Age 11, Children's Day School

One day, I was taking a bath while my mom scrubbed my fingernails. Suddenly, she looked at my arm, where my mole was. She started studying my mole.

"What is it?" I said absentmindedly.

"Oh, nothing," she said, but I could tell something was wrong by the tone of her voice.

Every once in a while, she would look at it with a worried expression. Finally, one day she said, "Today we are going to the doctor."

At the doctor's office, a woman in a white lab coat came to the door. "Elizabeth Levin," she said, "age eight. Dr. Aicardi is ready to see you."

As she led the way to room fifty-seven, I heard a baby cry. Then a thought struck me. *Was I getting a shot?* While I was waiting in the room, I looked at books. As the minutes ticked by, my head filled with questions. Why was my mom looking at my mole funny? Were they giving me a shot in my mole? Then Dr. Aicardi walked in. She looked at my mole. Then she said, "The skin doctor needs to take out your mole. It is light with dark blotches. I don't think it should be on your arm." I looked at her in disbelief.

About a month later, I found myself at the skin doctor's. I had come here a few times over the past couple of weeks and all they did was look at it and talk. Now it was the big day. I had a numbing patch on my mole and my American Girl doll, Samantha. I was ready. A woman called me in. She had me lie down on a padded table. A couple more doctors came in. My mom took off the patch, which didn't hurt. Then, my mom had me stick out the arm with the mole on it away from my body. "Don't look," she said. I turned my head the other way. As Samantha lay down next to me, my mom held my hand.

I waited for them to take the mole out. After a while, it dawned on me that I couldn't feel what they were doing, only occasional pricking. My mom said, "Done!" I looked down to where my mole used to be. I saw two black stitches! I didn't have the stitches for very long, but whenever I looked at them, it grossed me out to think of them sewing my skin. Oh well, at least I can say I have gotten a mole removed.

[*In a workshop entitled "How to Bring Down the House," taught by Micah Pilkington, a group of eleven- to fourteen-year-olds conquered territory that frightens most adults: they wrote autobiographical stories, then performed them in front of an audience. After hours of furious writing and some help from the Story Monkey, the class staged a reading for family, friends, and pirate store patrons that ended in applause. Thankfully, there was no structural damage to 826 Valencia.*]

Marriage

by MADISON PARKER

Age 12, Aptos Middle School

It was sometime during September, a warm sunny day. Too bad I couldn't enjoy it. That morning I had a huge bowl of sweet cereal, and it made me ill. Playing the flute in a stuffy classroom first period hadn't helped either. I called my mom because I knew she would come get me.

After waiting in the office, watching everyone else come in and out, my mom came. When I walked to the car, I saw a huge smile spread over her face. I knew it wasn't your average, everyday smile. When I got into the car, my mom immediately asked me if I wanted to be in a wedding.

"Whose?" I asked, for some reason dreading her saying "Mine," which was exactly what she did. At first, I had a cheesy "congrats" smile on. When we got home, I couldn't hold it in. I almost started crying. I wasn't really mad at her, though. I just thought things were going to be different.

I loved Tommy, and he had been living with us for a long time. That's when I realized everything was going to be the same, that this was a good thing. I was lucky to have so many people love me and care about me. Mostly I was mad because it was such a shock and a surprise. Then I got excited. Picking out the dresses and a place to have the reception—it was awesome. I got a brown dress with pink polka dots. It was very pretty. We picked out Chinese dresses for the wedding reception.

Finally, it was the day of the ceremony. It was also the day before Thanksgiving, a Wednesday. It was a school day, but I didn't go to school. Cousins, aunts, and close friends all flew in. We spent most of the day getting ready. I remember walking up the stairs of City Hall and seeing my grandparents waiting anxiously. First, my mother got registered and then we walked up the marble staircase to the top of the stairs. I remember being blinded by light from the flashes of the cameras. We waited around a little, and then it was time. My little sister and I stood next to them. I got a beautiful heart-shaped necklace. We got our pictures taken more. I remember the cold marble stairs. As we walked out, we saw Mayor Willie Brown going into the elevator. We jumped up and down the stairs and went up and down in the elevators. It was so much fun.

The next morning, we had to start really getting ready for the reception. All day long, people were running all over the house, in and out. Then we all got ready. We did our makeup and everything. When we got to the reception, there were lots of people showing up. The lights were up, and the disco ball was out. We danced all night. My uncle played music on his iPod. It was a night to remember.

It's been a few months now; I know this was a good thing. Nothing has changed.

[*In a workshop entitled "How to Bring Down the House," taught by Micah Pilkington, a group of eleven- to fourteen-year-olds conquered territory that frightens most adults: they wrote autobiographical stories, then performed them in front of an audience. After hours of furious writing and some help from the Story Monkey, the class staged a reading for family, friends, and pirate store patrons that ended in applause. Thankfully, there was no structural damage to 826 Valencia.*]

Amanda

by BRANDWIN STROUD

Age 12, Home-schooled

One year is a long time in itself. It is a long time to forget, a long time to remember, and a long time to grow up. It has, however, been more than a year, and the details of this story have gotten a little muddled.

A few years ago—three, I am willing to estimate—my brother and I got into an argument with my father. It does not matter what I did; what matters is the result. Dad came to a decision that would change everything. Here is where the story gets a little confusing. I know that he showed us a picture I thought was of Mom, and that we had a long talk about gender. As it turned out, Dad was transgendered.

Two percent of the American population is born with the body of one gender and the brain of another. Most transgendered people are disbelieved, and live a hard life because of it. Even though our community is lightening up, many transgendered people remain in the closet.

Dad quickly became a second mother. She shall remain anonymous so as to save her embarrassment, but, so that she has a name, I will call her Amanda. It took us a while to lose the male pronoun, and even longer to lose "Dad," but after a while everything settled down. After more time, all four of us moved in with my mother's boyfriend. The appearance of Dad as Amanda did not bother me, though when she started growing breasts I was a little surprised.

No one can really be blamed for this. My mother didn't know, and Amanda didn't have a choice. Blame it on whatever higher power you believe in, plural or singular, if you really must. I really didn't have a problem until I was assigned an Integrated Writing Assessment at school.

We were given the subject "An Event That Changed Your Life." I had plenty of time to think about it. I went over my cat, home-schooling, and Burning Man. I still didn't know what to write about.

A friend suggested that, since the teacher had told us everything would be kept secret, I should write about my dad—after all, I never mentioned him. I told her it was a great idea. She was kidding; I was not. I saw no reason not to. I trusted and respected the staff, and there was no child abuse involved. What did I have to lose?

During class, I used the subject of Amanda. I told no one. This was the first time I wrote about it, and writing requires thinking. I hadn't thought about it for three years. I made several painful motions to stop myself from crying, one of which was mistaken for raising my hand. I said nothing, and I did not cry. The period passed, and I lost no dignity.

There was a reason for this near-break. When you lie to yourself, it is usually because you do not want to believe the truth, or because the truth is difficult to believe. I had a situation that was, basically, both of the above. I was angry.

What Amanda did not realize is that she had changed. Men and women have very different personalities. When Dad was a woman pretending to be a man, she could not paint her nails, wear a dress, grow her hair out, or whatever else a normal woman would do. When Amanda stopped pretending to be a man, she did all those things and more. Another difference that hit me like a cannonball is that Amanda is bi and Dad was not. I had known about bi people for a while, so it did not bother me. But it was a difference, and I hated the differences. They made me yell and hit the wall with whatever was at hand, and then calm down until I was just crying quietly on my bed. For a while you would have thought it was my hobby.

Things settled back down maybe a month later, when I started paying attention to the other changes. Amanda might have been more self-centered and a lot more sensitive, but people never change in just one direction. She was also easier to talk to, supportive, helpful, and funny. She didn't care who I had a crush on; she supported me. She told me everything I showed her was fine, even if it was the worst thing she ever saw, and then told me how things could improve. She helped build tree forts. I could keep listing things forever.

[*In this workshop, taught by Laurel Newby and Renata Ewing, students ages eleven to six-
teen studied and then wrote using some of the traditional poetic forms such as the sonnet,
the villanelle, and the sestina. Students worked on their own poems as well as collaborative
group compositions. The workshop concluded with the publication of the student-written collection* A Poem for Each Blade of Grass.]

Selections from
A Poem for Each Blade of Grass

Raw Figure

by FIONA ARMOUR
Age 13, Herbert Hoover Middle School

Stitches roll up its arm, across its face,
to remember without a past, in a gate.
It sits taunted by the fatal song; in this place
Is the shelf, its only backbone, resembling its fate.

Cars, people, chattering like madmen,
enriched, it watches behind the
hole, clawing at the wind about its
buttons, tearing at its torn fabric 'til it bleeds.

Roaring until shadows can't make
fun of it, lying beneath a
blanket about its tears of stuffing, to take
about the only rip on its velvet tan.

The tunnel of its internal cage
gives off the only aura of a friend's shade.

Playing Games

by HELEN PORTER

Age 12, Home-schooled

A mess of laughter and yells.
A collapsed fort of blankets and pillows.
A little boy stands, and challenges me.

"Brothers," I say and narrow my eyes
"Sisters," he says and I laugh and go to join
The mess of laughter and yells.

I enter the fray and roll around,
Knowing full well I'll need to clean up. Then
A little boy stands, and challenges me.

I glare in mock hate, pick up a pillow,
And deal him a blow. For that's what you do in
A mess of laughter and yells.

A play sword is drawn, and suddenly
We stand, fighting desperately, but not really, I
    know.
A little boy stands, and challenges me.

I wrap myself in a blue cowboy blanket,
And suddenly it is my duty, and I stand
As a little boy stands, and challenges me
In a mess of laughter and yells.

Villanelle—In Her Mind

by Chandra Dawson

Age 13, Herbert Hoover Middle School

Her mind is her creation
Wherever she goes, her thoughts wander
While glances arouse suspicion

Cruel thoughts and neurotic memories
    are signs of desperation
Surrounding her, others ponder
Her mind is her creation

Running without a destination
She looks out into the yonder
While glances arouse suspicion

Filling her with trepidation
So much is beyond her
Her mind is her creation

Police start an investigation
Disguise makes her hair blonder
While glances arouse suspicion

Standing alone is her last confession
Her run becomes a saunter
While glances arouse suspicion
Her mind is her creation

Villanelle

by BRIGID MARTIN

Age 12, School of the Arts

How does that young girl sleep?
Her fist curled up near her cheek,
Her mother sings her a song of the deep.

The evening's fading fast;
The flag is set at half-mast.
How does that young girl sleep?

Her dreams are all locked in the attic
    without a sound,
While the nightmares seep up
    through the ground.
Her mother sings her a song of the deep.

The drums pound,
And violin's sound fades into a dream.
How does that young girl sleep?

The ending note rings in her ear,
And silently falls a salty, cool tear.
Her mother sings her a song of the deep.

And lastly as they take their bow,
The moon and sun clap for the girl.
Her mother sings her a song of the deep.
How does that young girl sleep?

Clement

by HELEN PORTER

Age 12, Home-schooled

Beg from me a smile,
I will comply with grace.
My heart leaps a mile
While I turn a blank face.

I take a deep breath, but every time I see you
I smooth out my hair and straighten my back.
My friends don't understand what I see in you
And that's fine with me, too.

They always ask me "why?" and "who?"
And I say you!
When you enter it's my cue
To blush and say hello, while my friends stand by
    and gloat.

You're like my branch of everlasting fire.
Your smile lifts me higher.

[About once every two months, data is collected as Andro Hsu, Amie Nenninger, and Jenny Traig lead a laboratory of parafictitious scientists (ages five to eight) conducting a series of experiments. Each student in the "Make-Believe Science" class learns to temporarily do away with facts, formulas, and the rules of physics in order to reach new creative heights.]

Scientific Formulae and Findings

HENRY MONTEIRO, *Age 6*; RIGO VALADEZ-BISLER, *Age 8*;
COLETTE ARO, *Age 8*; LAINE ARO, *Age 6*; SHIVANI BURRA, *Age 6*;
TEO VALADEZ-FLYNN, *Age 8*; ANTHONY CABRAL, *Age 6*;
NOAH MORTON, *Age 8*

On Physics

Our scientists observed objects that either sank or floated in water, and evaluated why:

Cork:
> *Floated*
> "It's very heavy, and heavy things float."

—Anthony

Toy zebra:
> *Sank and Floated*
> "It can swim, but when it doesn't swim it sinks."

—Colette

Chalk:
> *Floated*
> "Because it is white."

—Shivani

On Astronomy

Descriptions of Jupiter and its creatures:

Lots of cats. It's just like Earth, but everyone is a cat, including George Washington and Indians.

—Laine

No one can live on Jupiter, or they'd melt.

—Teo

It has little pieces of sand and when you step on them, they make sparks. Jupiter's creatures look a little different from all the creatures on this Earth. They have big ears, bigger than hippo or elephant ears. —Anthony

It looks like a chandelier with lightbulbs.

—Colette

(One scientist, Henry, saw Neptune instead of Jupiter, where he discovered "there are cities.")

On Anatomy

The digestive path of a piece of chocolate:

First, it goes to a shark. Then, it goes to the ocean, where I eat the shark. Finally, I hit the shark on the head, and he gives the chocolate back to me. —Anthony

It goes to your throat, where it goes down a super twisty slide. Then, it goes to your blood. —Noah

First, it goes to the throat, where it becomes strange and dissolves. Then, it goes to the intestines, where water goes onto it and

it becomes even more yummy. Finally, it goes to an animal (a real live giant) who passes it to the stomach, where it is crushed into tiny pieces.
—Henry

On Chemistry

Formulae:

Chicken + potato = a potato with wings and a beak
—Colette

Food + dirt = worms
—Teo

Sand + cruncher = glass
—Noah

Lick + tongue = lickatongue
—Rigo

At-Large Submissions

We receive quite a number of stories, poems, and essays—so many of them great—from young authors who live all over the United States. We welcome submissions; we love to read them and we publish as many as we can. We urge you, if you're under 18 years of age and have written something you really care about, to submit your work for publication. Email your submissions, with your full name, age, and the name of the school you attend, to quarterly@826valencia.com. If you prefer to send regular mail, our address is 826 Valencia St., San Francisco, CA 94110.

Goose

by TERESA COTSIRILOS

Age 15, College Preparatory School

Mommy had promised Phuong that they could bake a chocolate cake with green icing for Cam's eleventh birthday. They take Mommy to the hospital instead. Daddy drives, and Cam and Mama Thanh come, too. The hospital smells like acid and Windex. The walls of the hospital shine and gaze like eyes with no irises, and the people in the crisp, white robes smile down at Phuong with their big white teeth. "Hello little *girl*," they croon. "Your mommy's going to be A-O-K. Okay?" Phuong tries to retract her head into her neck like a telescope, but it doesn't work. She closes her eyes, but the white lights glow through her eyelids, and then she feels herself tip and slowly start to spin crookedly like a top about to fall. When she opens them the white faces are still there. They orbit above her in little white rings. "Don't be *scared*, little *girl*. Don't be *scared*."

"I'll keep 'em away," says Goose. She squeezes Phuong's wrist with her little hand, a hand with a palm the size of a bottle cap and five fingers thinner than spider legs. Phuong breathes in and she can smell Goose—that smell of melted chocolate. She feels a little better.

Goose is beautiful. She always wears a jade green dress, which

63

is Phuong's very favorite color. Her eyes are jade green, too. Her hair is black, a sheet of eclipsed sun that tickles the balls of her feet when she walks. Phuong found her behind the refrigerator two years ago, when Mommy first went to the hospital. "Just a check-up," they'd said.

Goose smiles encouragingly. Phuong juts out her bottom lip defiantly and glares at the infinite flock of white faces. "Go... away."

The white faces giggle and jiggle in place. "Oh, isn't she sweet," one of them says to Daddy. "She's so scared."

"Don't be *scared*," they chorus. "There's nothing to be *scared* of."

"I won't let 'em hurt you," Goose whispers. "I'll do the jabakadooza spell on them! I'll turn 'em into a bunch of old iguanas!"

"Leave us *alone*," Phuong says to the faces. "You hear me?"

"Your mommy's going to be just *fine*, little *girl*. Juuuuuuu*uust* fi*iiiiine*."

They wheel Mommy into the lobby. She's dressed in a big white shirt made of paper, and Phuong can see her skinny yellow legs, hanging listlessly like the chickens' feet in Mr. Tran's butcher shop downtown. Phuong lunges, but Mama Thanh pulls her back by a pigtail, and Mommy is wheeled away by the people in the crisp, white robes with the big, white teeth. Daddy goes with them. Phuong watches the wheelchair grow smaller and smaller. The white hall swallows, and Mommy is gone.

"Don't be scared," the faces say, and they circle closer, closer.

"I'll hold 'em off," Goose says and squeezes Phuong's hand a little tighter.

"Come on," says Cam. "Let's go home."

*　　*　　*

It's raining when they get to Mama Thanh's. "There are men playing drums in the sky," Goose tells Phuong, "and the other men are clapping. Hear it?"

"Yeah."

The dark, dank apartment smells like wet cats and tea, and the gray, funneled light is parched and stale. There are bodies propped silently against the caved paisley couch, on the peeling walls, and into the arthritic wicker chairs. The shadows shift as Phuong, Goose, Cam, and Mama Thanh shut the door behind them with a creak and snap. The bodies shift silently like shadows. The shadows shift flickering like souls.

"How's Lan?"

"She gonna be okay?"

"Where's Quan?"

"Dad's staying with Mom," Cam says. "He's staying the night, I think." He shrugs off his poncho, and the plastic crackles as he hangs it up.

The bodies move; the shadows hiss.

"Here, let me help you."

"Do you want tea?"

"Aya, this is terrible."

"You think this is the…"

"I hope not."

"How long you think it'll… be?"

"Let's go," says Goose.

Phuong follows her to Mama Thanh's room. She watches the balls of Goose's tiny feet pat up and down on the molting carpet, the sheet of her black hair swinging back and forth in whispers across the ground. The shadows snicker—"don't be scared, Phuong, don't be scared"—but Goose tells them to shut up or she'll do the jabakadooza spell on them. "I'll turn you into a bunch of avocados and eat you!" she bellows, and the shadows fall silent at her roar.

"I'm glad you're here, Goose," Phuong says softly. They sit down on Mama Thanh's bed.

"Thanks. Want chocolate?"

"Okay."

It rains harder. Lightning stencils the bed and dresser white, then dies to the deep rumbling of wheels. "That's the men in the sky having car races," Goose explains. "They keep flicking on and off their headlights, see."

"How do you know this stuff?"

"I just do."

They sit in quiet, savoring the chocolate. There are sepia photos in Mama Thanh's room of zigzagging streets and people in triangle hats. Mommy had once told Phuong they were pictures of a city called Saigon, where Mama Thanh lived a very long time ago. The pictures are hung in a collage across the walls, and the glass in their frames is always clean. "Let's go there," Goose says. "It looks sunny."

"Okay!" Phuong takes Goose's hand, careful not to crush the spider leg fingers. They start to spin, faster and faster and faster until they land in the streets with the people in triangle hats shouldering by. It smells like sweat and pee and people.

Goose shades her eyes. "We should've brought sunglasses."

Phuong grins. "Come on—let's go ride the bus! I heard Daddy talk about them—people get to ride on the *roof!*"

"Oh boy!"

They ride the bus, and then they buy ice cream. Then they ride the bus and eat their ice cream. Goose almost falls off the bus, but Phuong catches her. At night, they sit on the bus and watch the cataracts of city lights. At midnight, there are fireworks that snap and boom and crack and bloom and—

"Phuong?"

Goose and Phuong are back on Mama Thanh's bed. Cam is standing in the doorway. "Phuong?" he says. He rigidly walks into the bedroom, like a robot with a low battery.

"Yeah?"

"Phuong I… look." He rubs his face.

"What is it, Cam?" Goose asks.

"Yeah," says Phuong, "what is it?"

"Phuong," he says, "I…"

And then he sits on Goose.

Goose shrieks, and her jade eyes bulge like they're being pushed from the inside of their sockets by thumbs. Cam has sat directly on her stomach, and he doesn't get up.

"Stop it!" Phuong yells. "Get off her!"

Cam's eyebrows vee and he looks around him at the bed. "What?"

Goose can't breathe. She's beating at Cam's back with her palms, but they're the size of bottle caps, and he doesn't feel it. "Get off her!" Phuong screams. "You're sitting on Goose!"

Cam gets up. His nose accordions. "Goose?"

Phuong violently points at Goose. "Goose, you stupid-head, Goose!"

"What are you—Phuong, I—I… look, need to tell you—"

"Cam," Goose croaks. She's clutching her stomach, fingering her ribs.

"Goose! Goose! You sat on her! I hate you!"

"Phuong," he snaps, "there's nothing there."

Goose's lip quivers. "What?" She covers her ears with her hands.

Phuong hiccups. "Don't be scared, Goose! Don't be scared!"

"Phuong, *listen*—"

"No."

"Christ—look, can I sit *down* now?"

"No!"

"There's nothing friggin' *there*—"

"Do the jabakadooza spell!" Phuong cries desperately, but Goose is covering her ears with her tiny hands and shaking her head, shaking her head.

"'Kay, you know what?" Cam sits. The bedsprings creak. Goose cries.

Phuong is crying, too. She tries to hit him, but Cam is so much bigger. "Stop it!" she's screaming. "Stop!"

Cam's eyes are overbright, and they hold Phuong's gaze with the gravity of stars. "Say it."

"What?"

"She's not even real! Say it!"

"I hate you!" Goose is crying. Phuong looks into her stricken face and realizes that she's looking through it. "Don't be scared, Goose!" Phuong bleats. "Don't be scared! It'll be okay—Cam, get off! Get *off*!"

"I'll get up if you say she's not real."

"I *hate* you!"

"I will—just say it."

The tears make Cam look slurred and out of focus, like when Phuong wears Daddy's glasses. She swallows. "She's... she's..." She buries her head in her knees. "Go away!"

Cam looks at everything but her, then gets up, stiffly. There is nothing left but wrinkled sheets where he was sitting. "If crap like that—was real," he gasps and stabs a finger in Phuong's face. "This wouldn't have happened on my birthday." He leaves. His shoulders are rolled like an old man's.

Phuong jumps off the bed. "Goose!" she cries. "Goose, come back!"

But all that's left is the faint smell of chocolate, the moats of shadows, and an avalanche of rain.

Business Is Business

by REÜBEN PÖLING

Age 17, School of the Arts

Mallory's was a successful bar and a very nice place to drink in. The stools were upholstered in tasteful, comfortable, dark green leather, and the bar was made of polished, stained wood. The tables were small—either private and intimate or open and public depending on how far you leaned in. The lighting was pleasantly dim, and the atmosphere was welcoming overall. A jukebox currently playing the Eagles provided a soundtrack for a generally cheerful and somewhat plump bartender of forty-two, about twenty human customers at stools and tables, and a devil and an angel sitting at the corner table.

Out of all of these features, the devil and the angel are likely the most interesting, unless you are an upholsterer, an obsessive Eagles fan, or a follower of college football (in which case you would be interested in the Michigan State wide receiver and his girlfriend at one of the other tables). If you are one of those types, then perhaps you would be better served reading another story. Otherwise, you will hopefully be satisfied with the devil and the angel.

They met at Mallory's every month or so to drink and talk. They were enemies, of course, on opposite sides of the great war that consumed all creation. But they were also friends, though neither completely trusted the other. Every month, the devil would discuss what his side had been up to, the angel would reciprocate, and both of them would make notes to counter certain of each other's plans, appearing thus to be accomplishing something. It had been the devil's idea.

It should be noted, for the sake of clarity, that the devil was not exactly a devil. He was actually a god—a fairly powerful god, in fact—of a pantheon worshipped fervently by Scandinavian pirates (in the old days) and smelly, long-haired teenagers (in more current times). But because he was *a* Power of Evil, though not *the* Power of Evil, it is convenient to refer to him as a devil. He had neatly trimmed red hair and a neatly trimmed red goatee, mild sea-green eyes, and thin white scars around his lips. He wore an expensive-looking dark blue suit and smiled a great deal. His name was Loki. He was drinking a Pilzen, with a shot glass of amaretto close at hand.

The angel, on the other hand, was just that—an angel, also powerful. His hair was a very pale blond, and worn in a ponytail. His eyes were rich brown, matching his jacket and khakis. He had a slightly worried air about him; his movements would have been furtive if they were not so graceful. His name was Raphael. He was drinking a Guinness.

The devil, at the moment, was talking. He talked a great deal. "And then, like a fool, the giant just hands the hammer over. The whole time I'm thinking, *By Niflheim itself, there's no way he could be missing the beard.* But he missed the beard—he seriously thought the mighty Thor was a woman. Can you imagine that kind of stupidity, Ralph?"

"So what did Thor do then?" asked Raphael. He didn't remember this story, though Loki had probably told it to him at some point in the past. Even Loki ran out of new stories eventually.

"What do you think he did? He had his hammer. He pulled off the veil, stood up, and smashed the big idiot's head in. Then he rampaged around—in a bridal dress, mind you—crushing giants left and right. The whole time, I'm just sitting there practically piss-ing myself, tripping a giant every now and then, watching Thor storm around killing giants with a dress on!" Loki laughed. "You know Thor—imagine that scene. Just imagine it." Raphael imagined it and chuckled. "So remind him of that next time he starts being an ass. He does that a lot."

"I don't know, Thor always struck me as a pretty decent fellow." The angel was being honest, of course—as a Power of Good, he could only lie for a good cause. There was no good cause around to lie for, so he could no more lie about Thor than contend that the bartender could fly. The bartender could lie about Thor all he wanted, though, so it sort of worked out in the end.

"Oh sure, he's a very nice guy," said Loki, a bit sarcastically. "He's a great guy; he'd give you the shirt off his back if you asked for it. The peasants loved him. Everybody sacrificed to him at least once a week. They loved him, almost as much as they loved that damn kid Balder." As he spoke the last four words, his mild eyes went hard and his hair seemed to brighten. The wide receiver sitting three tables over glanced at them briefly, but decided their conversation was none of his business and turned away.

"Sounds like it could get a bit irritating," said Raphael hastily, before Loki could really get started on one of his rants. He could very comfortably go on for hours about his loathing for the Norse god of light. "But you need somebody to swing the hammer around, right?"

"Yeah, sure. And he was pretty good at that," conceded Loki, visibly defusing. "I mean, he took out a wedding's worth of giants in a dress. I gotta give him credit for that. And he was a good guy to travel with. Awful cook, though."

Raphael nodded. They sat in silence for a second as the Eagles song ended. Next was the Electric Light Orchestra. Identical expressions of revulsion crossed the devil's pale face and the angel's tan one, and Loki turned and stared at the jukebox. His eyes lit up, but not in a very pleasant way, and the music abruptly slowed and stopped. The jukebox began to smoke.

"You know, you didn't have to do that," said Raphael. "I could have just changed the song. They have 'Mr. Taxman' on that juke-box." Loki and Raphael didn't agree on all that many things, as devils and angels in general agreed on very few. But one of the things that just about all of them agreed on was The Beatles. Similarly, excluding a handful of devils with a penchant for caus-ing true agony, they all agreed on the Electric Light Orchestra.

Loki waved his hand dismissively. "I spared these poor people from the Electric Light Orchestra forever. It was an act of Good—you should be proud."

Raphael didn't argue with that. "Wasn't that band one of yours?"

The devil nodded in dismay. "They were Beelzebub's idea. He's a real bastard. I mean, even by my standards."

Raphael nodded in agreement. "My side's made our share of mistakes. Communism was supposed to be our big push for world peace and equality."

"Wow, that one worked really well."

"Tell me about it. And—you'll get a kick out of this one—the Allfather was supposed to pick the fellow to finish fixing that mis-take and kick-start world peace. You know who he picked?" Loki shook his head. "Ronald Reagan."

Loki burst out laughing. "You're crapping me! Odin picked *that* moron? Ohhh, that's beautiful!" His laughter slowly subsided. None of the humans in the bar paid much attention to the red-haired businessman cackling about some old pagan god. "Wow, first I trick him into surrendering the Norse pantheon to subor-dinate positions in Good and Evil, and then he picks Ronny Reagan as a champion of peace. I think he's getting senile in his old age."

Raphael shook his head. "I'm not so sure. Reagan seemed like an honest man, but he turned out to be kind of a hostile moron. It wasn't the fault of anyone on our side." Loki listened with his eyes narrowed, pondering this. "And I'm not just making excuses… I'll admit we should have looked better. But still, take Communism—

it was a good system, but humanity butchered it with greed. Hell, going all the way back to the Son—He preached love and forgiveness, and then after humanity killed Him they took His creed and turned it into an excuse for murder and hatred."

"I think that was flawed from the beginning, personally," observed Loki. "If you ask me, nobody wants to hear some dead Jew on a stick telling them to turn the other cheek. If people get hurt, they want revenge. Your side seems to forget that an awful lot."

"That's *exactly* my point!" said Raphael decisively. "We spend all this time planning and organizing, and we forget that we're fighting over the souls of a bunch of bastards! Humans can mess up anything we do, no matter how well designed it is, because we design it for basically good souls. And that's *not* the target audience."

Loki shook his head, smiling slightly. "I wouldn't say that, my friend. If they were as evil as all that, my side would have won a long time ago. I mean, hell, we've been meeting in this area for millennia, and the war's stayed even the whole time."

Raphael was already shaking his head again, his face flushed with drink. It is worth noting that angels get tipsy very quickly and stay that way for many more drinks, whereas devils generally do not feel the effects of alcohol until they suddenly find it very difficult to remain standing. "No, Loki, you don't see the point. We've got to fight against your machinations, put all our strength behind a few good humans. But you, you just drop a few hints and there's a million men and women ready to follow any hellish madness."

A couple of women at the next table looked over curiously. Loki sighed. "Ralph, you're drunk. Look, why don't we both go home? I'll meet you here again next month; we'll keep each other updated. You're talking like a damn lunatic. Humans have a lot of possibility, we both know that but—"

"No, no, don't interrupt me. I think I'm onto something—we need to change our way of thinking entirely. We need to…" Raphael's voice trailed off. "You know, I really shouldn't be telling you this."

"We really shouldn't be meeting without trying to kill each other, my friend," said Loki. "But what are you saying here? Your main point is…"

"That heaven is doing things all wrong because humanity just isn't equipped to handle a plan of basic Good. They're just way too effin' evil, too easily tempted by Evil."

Loki narrowed his eyes, a smile dancing behind his curious expression. "But that's just a fact of nature, not a mistake. I mean, there's nobody who could have known man would turn out to be flawed."

"God knew," was Raphael's automatic response. It should be taken into account that Raphael was somewhat drunk, and that Loki had always been a master at games of deceit. Hopefully, the reader, thus informed, will forgive the angel for those two words— for someone else certainly didn't.

Raphael suddenly was consumed by a fit of coughing, and his body began to shudder. Loki rose from his chair and hoisted Raphael up, then dragged him towards the men's restroom, drawing a few stares from the rest of the bar. The devil dragged the spasming angel into the facilities, shut the door, and leaned against it. He watched with some curiosity as white, pearl-feathered wings sprouted from his drinking buddy's back, then began to steam and wither away. Raphael's skin turned nearly pure gold, then darkened. Something unpleasant was happening to his basic bone structure, and white light shined from his eyes… but not for long.

"HOLY JESUS!" came a shout from the left. Loki winced at the sound of the name and turned to regard a buzz-cut young man standing beside one of the urinals, staring in shock at the floor. He moved his gaze to the devil and former Norse god. "What the eff is going on here? Who the hell are you? And what's wrong with—" he looked back down at the floor. "*OhholyGodcrapJesuseffno*—"

Loki stepped across the bathroom floor and put his hands on the gibbering man's shoulders, blocking his view of the thing on the floor. "Everything's going to be all right," he promised in a soft voice. The man looked into his eyes, just beginning to burn red, and the two held the stare for about ten seconds as Loki's eyes got brighter and brighter. Then the devil let go, and the man slumped to the floor where he stared catatonically into space, drooling.

Loki ignored him and looked at the floor, where something unspeakably hideous was staring up at him. It spoke with a voice that sounded like a thousand madmen screaming for blood. "What... what happened?"

"You questioned His will, Ralph. Remember what He does to angels who find fault with His plans?" The thing on the floor closed three eyes, none of which were in the right place for an eye, and gripped what was more or less a forehead in something that was not so much a hand as an assortment of natural weapons.

"No. Oh, you bastard. You set me up."

"Sorry, my friend. Business is business." Loki shrugged, then turned his back without fear and walked toward the door. Raphael attempted to rise and lunge at him, but something wasn't working. He had no clue how to utilize this utterly unfamiliar, freakish body. Meanwhile, Loki opened the door. What lay on the other side was not Mallory's, but a long, dark passageway lit only by human torches that flailed and screamed as they burned.

"Let's go, Ralph. Put your monkey suit back on—time to meet the management." Loki made a cellphone appear in his hand, dialed three digits, and said, "Success. I'm coming in." He then stepped aside. "Go ahead. You first." The cellphone had somehow become a knife, ancient and shining with power.

Raphael put his human form back on with a thought and rose shakily, still weak. He looked at Loki, his face alight with rage. He looked at the knife in Loki's hand. He looked at the door.

And because there was really nothing else he could do, he stepped through.

As Neruda's Messenger

by AMELIA ROSENMAN

Age 17, Lick-Wilmerding High School

FIRST INSPIRATION:
After watching *Amélie* at the Clay Street theatre, midnight on New Year's Eve, I knew I wanted to be Amélie Poulain. I wanted to don an umbrella and an accent and metamorphize into that secretive miracle-maker of Montmartre. I wished for the screen to stretch up and out and become a mirror.

SECOND INSPIRATION:
I have this deck of cards that's missing the ten of clubs.

THIRD INSPIRATION:
Pablo Neruda wrote a book of poems, all in the form of questions. He writes with such musical urgency, I want to whisper his lines to strangers.

MY PLAN:
Write Neruda's question-poems on the backs of each of the cards in my unfull deck. Distribute the cards in thematically appropriate locations. Hope that strangers will discover them and email me their reactions.

IN PREPARATION:
I set up a new email account. I try to think of clever names. Fiftyonecards? Questioner231? Iamnotastalker? I settle on missing-card@hotmail.com. I am satisfied. Unfortunately, I enter a faux zip code that does not match my faux state. After some finagling, the account is complete.

I spend an hour with the deck of cards, white paper, rubber cement, scissors, and pen. I am accompanied by the folk music stylings of Loreena McKennit. Here is what a sample card looks like:

Front: Six of hearts
Back: Con las virtudes que olvide, ¿me puedo hacer un traje nuevo?
With the virtues that I have forgotten, could I sew a new suit?
[Send questions and/or answers to: missingcard@hotmail.com]

PHASE ONE: ON PLANTING
POEM-CARDS IN FRONT YARDS
I sweep my neighborhood in Dickensian coat and scarf, my head held high. I reach into my pocket for a card that asks, "Why not give a medal to the first golden leaf?" More than half of the poems about nature involve the color yellow. I picture Neruda's hometown glowing yellow all year. I realize that I am prejudiced against ugly houses with ugly trees. I favor houses with brightly colored doors and dazzling Japanese maples. The most beautiful trees have luminous red leaves that dare the sky to glory its blue through their branches.

There is one house on Aragon that smells like someone sprayed it with green tea house-cologne. The house next door smells like gasoline. I find both distasteful. One man pulls up in his car just as I slide a card into his mailbox. I avoid eye contact. His mailbox reminds me of a reptile's mouth.

PHASE TWO: CHEZ LES FLORISTES
There are eleven people working at the florist's, a shop of approximately two hundred square feet. These are busy gardeners, and

merry. Two women shout to each other over watering cans about the droopiness of their daffodils. They are blond, kerchief-wearing women, one stout and one long. A bearded man claws mounds of dirt from a bucket into a cardboard crate. He scratches his cheek. I watch the other workers pump their spray bottles with importance. The few customers furrow their brows at pale roses.

I worry immediately that there are too many eyes for me to accomplish my task. Surely someone will spot me, a fraudulent shopper. She is not here to purchase! She will buy nothing! Fire! (They spray me with many hoses.)

In truth, I am invisible. I deposit my king and queen of hearts right beneath their dripping gloves. No one even asks if I need help. It's a tad insulting. The cards I leave speak of chrysanthemums, carnations, and: "Is there a star more open than the word poppy?" I drop them in flowerpots and imagine the lucky customer who will shake one dry in her kitchen, clippers in hand.

PHASE THREE: WHERE ARE THE POMEGRANATES?

Should I take a shopping basket? Why would I take a shopping basket? I am not shopping. I will put nothing in the basket. The empty basket will give me away. The lack of basket will give me away more. I take a basket.

My first card for the grocery store asks: "How do the oranges divide up the sunlight in the orange tree?" There is a man by the oranges, squeezing them like breasts. I do not want this man to see my card. I will stare at the persimmons until he leaves. The skin of a persimmon will cut your throat if you swallow it. The man is gone. (He is licking his lips. He is grotesque.) I slide my card, the four of clubs, between two tangerines, which are not oranges, but look like them.

The next card is something about vodka and lightning bolts. Do they have security cameras here? I am underage and furtive around the hard liquor. I can imagine the scene:

Loudspeaker: Shoplifter in aisle three! Shoplifter in aisle three!

Breadstacker (breathing hard): All right, give it up.

Me: What?

Breadstacker: We can't have you stealing wine.

Me: I haven't stolen anything.

Breadstacker: Come here.

Me: You can't pat me down! You stack bread!

Breadstacker: You just come here, little lady. Do you have something to hide?

I slip the card between two bottles and am on my way.

Should I put something in my basket so I look like I'm buying something? I have no money, but what if someone is suspicious? I am doing nothing wrong. These are gifts; these are saviors; these are miracles I am dispensing. Right.

I plant the three of diamonds beneath a loaf of rye: "When the color yellow runs out, with what will we make bread?" This is a personal favorite. I can imagine the yellow paint drying and cracking, the bread of the world crumbling collectively.

My final stop is at the pomegranates. Reading the poem, you can feel the fruit's blood on your hands. I do not find the pomegranates. There are seeded grapes, unseeded grapes, blackberries, blueberries, strawberries, even juniper berries, for god's sake!

There are pineapples, cantaloupes, honeydews, watermelons, kiwis; California's multi-seasonal agricultural splendor spreads itself before me. But no pomegranates. The lonely, fingernail-staining fruit of the gods is absent. I slide the card between some raspberries, which have a similar hue. All is well.

I ditch the basket craftily behind some tulips. I stride out of the store, smiling at an important woman in a black apron who looks above my head.

FINAL PHASE: GIRL ON A TRAIN

Here I fulfill my Amélie fantasy. I stare at my fellow BART passengers. We are all silent and nose-snuffing. I try to make eye contact with a few people, then stop for fear of sending stalker-like vibes. I will leave the remaining cards here, on seats in various cars. I will zoom into the city and zoom back, peering at the numbers carved in the tunnels when the train slows. I try stuffing one card between armrest and seat. It slides down and I have to plunge my hand in after it—my knuckles burn. I snatch the card. I wonder if the BART cleaning crew will pick up my cards and trash them without reading. I hope they do not. I think of handing one card to the woman who pets her child by the door. She would under-stand. She would not reject the card. I can't do it. I don't want to. I can't. I think: What if other people started copying me, leaving cards with messages all over the subway? The *Chronicle* could write a human interest story about us: "Mysterious Message Spreaders Astound BART Riders," or better: "Prescient Playing Cards Plague the Underground." That has a nice ring to it. The journalists would exit the train.

AND THEN AFTER EVERYTHING:

Bicycling home, I spot a few of my cards left in trees like leaves in hair. Wheeling down the sidewalk I feel like I am a maple farmer, checking my buckets. Once home, I log on to my new email account every fifteen minutes or so. There is a "Welcome to Hotmail" note that excites me unnecessarily. There is a letter I wrote to myself from my other email address. I am not surprised, but my breath sighs its disappointment. I will wait. I will keep checking. I have a few cards left, which I carry in my purse. I will leave one beneath my girlfriend's pillow. I will send one along with my brother who is driving hundreds of miles tonight. I will keep another in my pocket for my hand to reach and rub between my fingers.

The Bay Area Had Been Closing in on Her

by OLIVER SINAIKO

Age 18, Charter High School

The Bay Area had been closing in on her. It had become oppressive. The feeling that Barbara was being watched at all times overwhelmed her. She lived at the center of the action and had grown tired, no, exhausted, of it all. She was a size two, which was small. She was, in fact, thin. But within her thinness she had grown soft. When David touched her he either felt bone or fluff. Her strength, post-ballet, had disappeared. She realized she had probably been very good; that it was ridiculous for her ever to have stopped dancing; that her calves had grown weak with driving; that she now needed her glasses at all times; that she needed to renew her prescription and should consider contacts or even Lasik eye surgery.

Escaping the Bay Area did not have the intended effect, either. She still felt, when she left, as if she were being watched. San Franciscans were everywhere. She could not take a ski trip with her family or a quiet weekend with her husband without running into people. She couldn't leave—and yet, she had defined a need now, to leave. Leave or change her circumstances.

Barb was a Noe Valley mother. She wore clogs out to dinner and was a member of the Noe Valley Democratic Club. She kept a

Matt Gonzalez sign up in her window even after Newsom had won the mayoral race. She drove a Volvo with the cold weather package and she hated the thing. She hated her predicament. She hated Smith & Hawken and hated planting bulbs in the spring. But she also hated winter. She hated the lack of fall—leaves continuing to battle the elements through December, getting impossibly stuck to the cracked pavement in front of the house (removing them took swift and vigorous movement with a small push broom, back and forth, until they were all in the gutter).

Barb hated gourmet cooking and the time it consumed and the new expectation of both husband and children that she cook gourmet *every* night now. This she especially hated. It was enough, she thought, to volunteer weekly at her children's school. She thought it was enough to keep her family's life organized. She thought it was enough to keep everyone in comfortable under-wear and socks and organic food, but it wasn't. They wanted that toy or this dinner. They disagreed on whether or not the flowerbeds she had planted in the garden last summer looked nice. They wanted their toys put away for them.

So, she wanted to leave, really. She wanted to escape neighbor-hood chats with Frank Grant about how wonderful his new Labrador was. She wanted to escape the compulsory conversations that took place with Kate McCourt about her new Saab, how it was a good choice. She wanted, no, *needed*, to escape.

Her connection with her children was minimal. They wanted to quit soccer and play ball in the house. They wanted to be ghosts for Halloween and did not want to pick up their clothes. They did not want to put on their seatbelts. So, this was the situation. Barbara Schwartz: enforcer of rules. This was, at the same time, the role David Schwartz rejected with all his might.

David was fun and exciting. He took the kids to his office and let them make as many copies as they wanted in the copy room. They made friends with his secretary and fingerprinted the floor-to-ceiling windows of his corner office. He was a patent attorney.

This entitled him to late nights in the office and jogging early in the mornings. Barb had had a nothing job. She had known it was nothing for a while before she quit. She was a graphic designer at a small advertising firm in San Francisco. *Ms. Magazine* was not correct: she could not have her cake and eat it, too. She had children and began arriving late to the office. She began being late to important appointments because Jacob had the chicken pox or Andrew had been crying all morning. Then came the humiliation: the bottom-feeder jobs that no one wanted. These included designing ads for the local veterinary clinics, invitations to charity benefits and brochures for fiberglass Jacuzzis. Then, she quit. She decided to stay at home with the plan to go back in a year, then two, then three. It had now become someday. Someday she would return to work.

Barbara, of course, hated thinking about these things. She hated giving up dancing and working and independence. This brought her back to why she was doing what she was presently doing: making a harvest salad from typical vegetables of late fall. These included squash and carrots, lots of greens, etc. She had gotten the recipe from David's mother, a frail little woman who lived in the hills of Piedmont and had two little white dogs. She was widowed and loved to tell everyone how fond she was of her daughter-in-law. So, she emailed Barbara recipes and helped her with anything the little five foot two skeleton could get her hands on. In any case, Barbara chopped away at the harvest vegetables to escape these truths, these realities that flooded her mind at times of self-reflection.

"Barb!" David bellowed, making the very frame of the ancient house shake with trepidation for his next shout. "Barb? You here?" His voice caused some mix of resentment and anger to bubble beneath her skin. She hated him and yet, sometimes, she liked him. She liked him when they were making love. She liked him when she saw him, dripping with sweat, after a run. She liked him when he fixed things and liked it when he chuckled (though hated his laugh). So she did not hate him. She did like him sometimes.

"In the kitchen!" Barbara cried. David came galloping down the stairs and into the kitchen.

"Oh god, that smells good." He dropped his coat on the table that was pushed against a set of french doors no longer in use. "What's for dinner?" Barbara looked away.

"Well, I'm making some good stuff." She said this with the gusto of a great chef. "I'm cooking lamb chops and making a harvest salad."

David fell into a chair, "I can't wait." He grinned an awful grin. A grin, Barbara thought, that signified a sort of satisfaction with it all. He opened up a different set of french doors and stepped out to the gray night. It was December 20th and it was cold and dark and lonely.

"Please close the door!" Barbara cried. He pretended not to hear. "Please close the door." She was helpless. Still no reaction. She stomped over to the door in her flowing floral skirt and heavy clogs, bangs swinging. She smacked the two doors shut. She wanted to lock them.

David turned around and gave her a bewildered, betrayed look. He rushed to the doors as she returned to the center island and her chopping. "What was with that?" he cried. "Why? I don't understand, why? What the hell is going on?"

She rested her elbows on the center island. She looked up from her chopping and clenched her knife. "I was cold. I asked and you did not hear. No big deal." She looked down.

David slammed the doors behind himself now. "Oh, eff that crap, Barb. What the eff? I came home, completely pleasant, and you effin' slam the door on my back for no goddamn reason but your hot head." He moved toward her.

"Oh, forget you, really, David. I was cold, you butthole. I was cold and you were outside and you didn't bother to listen to me and that was that, really." Barbara dropped her knife on the butcher block. "I deserve to do my work, my cooking, here, the way I want."

David's jaw gaped open at her remarks, "Okay, fine, you know what…"

Someone was banging on the front door. Barbara left the argument. She looked out and saw Jayne Sherman delivering her children. Barbara flung the door open. Her children stood there, Andrew and Jacob, eight and ten respectively. "Well, hello." She looked down at her two little idiots in their matching rain slickers and curly, blonde little mops, then up to Jayne.

"Thanks, Jayne." Jayne was the type to wear hemp pants and loosely fitting knit sweaters.

"No problem, Barb. Hey, are you doing the parents' potluck thing?"

"Uh, ya know, I don't think so."

"Oh? Why not?"

Barbara hated Jayne and the way Jayne always acted as if Barbara were not living up to her responsibilities if she didn't go to every single function. She wanted to cry, "Because I don't effin' feel like it!"

"Oh, well, I am so busy. You know how it goes," Barb said.

Jayne was looking away now, back down towards her Subaru Outback (L.L. Bean Edition). "We're gonna miss you."

Barbara shuffled her kids into the house. "Mom, what's for dinner?" little Andrew asked as he stumbled into the home office underneath the staircase (really a converted windowless closet).

"A salad and lamb chops."

He booted up the iMac. "Oh, god. I hate lamb chops." He clicked on the icon for whatever his favorite game was (some game where you build cities and try to sustain them, but despite all efforts they eventually fall apart). "What's for dessert?"

She leaned on the center console in the entry hall, "Ice cream."

She could tell he had just rolled his eyes, "Mom, ice cream is not a dessert."

She began walking towards the kitchen. "Well, then, nothing," she replied.

"God, Mom. Relax. I don't care," he yelled back to her.

She returned to her chopping, throwing more vegetables into a large, stainless steel salad bowl. David, of course, had not moved. "So really, what's been with you lately?" he asked.

"Nothing. We can discuss this later, okay?"

"Well, I just don't understand why you would—"

"Later, alright?"

David looked down, "Okay."

Barbara continued chopping and working in the kitchen; it took her an hour and a half. "Okay, everybody. Time for dinner."

Two boys and a man came in stomping down the stairs. "Here, I'll help," David offered. He brought several plates into the french country dining room with its faux-weathered breakfront dining table, a mixture of warm wood finishes and chipped white paint. A large, silken chandelier hung from the ceiling, mocking the grandeur this middle-class home lacked.

All around the table, they sat. David and Barbara at their respective ends and the boys on either side sandwiched between dining chairs. Their meals all in front of them. "Oh, god, this is so gross," Jacob cried.

"Well, you don't have to eat it."

He dropped his fork, "I don't want to."

She took her first bite, "That's fine. No ice cream."

He slumped down in his Italian silk chair. "I don't care. Ice cream isn't a dessert."

When Barbara was a child ice cream was a rarity, not just a dessert but a special one, at that. "That's fine. No ice cream for a week."

David decided to intervene, "Okay. That's enough. Jacob, eat or go to your room." Jacob looked at his father, "Fine. I'll eat."

Contrary to what David had claimed, it had nothing to do with one's approach. "Just lay out their options and trust them to make the right decision," David had said. This was not true at all, of course. The fact was that their father was glamorous. He drove a BMW and drove it fast. He laughed with them and rough-housed. He smiled. He was never at home. So the woman who drove the Volvo, was always at school, and made them do their homework and brush their hair was terrible. She was mean and no one liked her.

They all finished their meals in low conversation around the table. It was dull. Andrew went to the computer and began playing his game again. Barbara walked by the makeshift office, with its recessed lighting and framed poster of a large-toothed African symbol that read "February 16–March 12, 1988" on the first line, and, on the next, "The Boston Museum of Folk Art."

"Andrew, where is your homework?"

"Mom, please. I am *trying* to play a game and you are very distracting."

"Andrew, have you done your homework? It's getting late. Just pause your game, please."

"I can't pause it online."

"Then tear yourself away for just a moment." She hated this.

"Fine. What? I did my homework."

"Let's see."

"I did it."

"Okay, fine. Show me."

He pulled his blue Jansport backpack onto his lap. He fumbled inside the bag until he found a crumpled piece of paper. It was covered in double-digit division and multiplication—all complete-ly correct.

"Is this all your homework?"

"Yes." He returned to the computer. Then this, just a small whisper: "Get a life."

"What?"

"Nothing."

She yanked him off the chair as he struggled to get loose. She pulled him across the entry hall and into the kitchen. "Forget this crap," she muttered. She flung open a set of french doors (the same

set she had slammed on her husband before). She pushed him outside. Locked the door. "Listen," she said from inside. "I'm tired of
this crap. So just stay the hell out there and freeze for five minutes."

Andrew kicked the door, cracking a pane of glass. Then he fell
to the ground and cried. Barbara, of course, automatically opened
the door. "Oh, god." She brought him to his feet, "Maybe Mommy
got too angry. Maybe we both did."

She held him while he pushed away. "I hate you."

She stepped back for a moment. "Now, you can't really say
that, Andy."

Crossing his arms, he looked away, at a wind chime blowing
around in the breeze outside. "No, I do."

Barbara wondered in bed that night if Andrew truly hated her.
She knew parents were not supposed to take things like this seriously, not at all. But, she wondered still if he hated her. Her sole
purpose in life was to send these children in the opposite direction
of whatever their natural inclinations told them. They wanted
sweet; she gave them hearty. They wanted play; she gave them
work. They wanted messy; she wanted neat. Her job was to beat
them down until they gave in to work and hearty food and neat-
ness—until they felt as if they could not live any other way. She fell
asleep thinking about this.

*　　*　　*

At 6:45 a.m. Barbara woke in her room—fifteen minutes before
schedule. This allowed her to indulge in the fact that here, now, she
was independent. She crept across the master bedroom and down
the front stairs and opened up the *San Francisco Chronicle* with its
fluff pieces and endless typos. Here, she read on the first page about
a massive blackout that occurred last night leaving a third of the
city in the dark. Also, cooler temperatures with intermittent show-
ers on the way for the five days to come. No school today for the
boys (but they did have soccer which regularly took place in the
rain) and David had work (today was his last day before the holi-

days). Also, it was the shortest day of the year—a day in which primitive tribes around the world rejoiced; for what godforsaken reason, Barbara had no idea.

She wrapped herself tightly in her cotton bathrobe and turned up the heat in the house to seventy-five in stark contrast with the forty-four degree morning. People in the house began to wake up and come down the stairs. She prepared breakfast (Grape Nuts—preparation included the placing of milk, the box, and bowls on the kitchen table). She sat, her robe wrapped as tightly as possible around her and her thick, heavy bangs falling in her eyes. They all came in, one by one.

First, Andrew: "Sorry, Mom. I'm really sorry I got so mad." He had learned already the act of appeasement. She accepted and waited for Jacob to sit at the table. Both boys could pour their own cereal.

Then David. He came down and poured coffee for himself (their machine was self-brewing). "Well, gotta run. See you all tonight." With that, he was gone. He and Barbara had never finished their talk. The sun was to set today before five o'clock. The morning was still dark. Soccer was in one hour.

So, Barbara did laundry. She arranged a vet appointment for Roscoe. She made another appointment for a tune-up for the BMW. Then she wrapped presents in a finished basement room while the boys busied themselves above her in the rest of the house. She found this methodical wrapping calming; this calm, perhaps, was at the heart of her troubles. All that she chose to do was methodical and calming; it was the plight of the Noe Valley mother. Gardening, gift-wrapping, soccer parties, shopping, gourmet cooking, and yoga: it was all work veiled in recreation. She felt as if she did nothing and had lost her balance in life. It was always fighting, arguing, and pleading or wrapping, drying, and stretching. It was an endless stream of melancholy extremes.

She took the boys to soccer in the rain. They were strapped tightly to the back seat of the Volvo wagon (silver, leather upholstery and looked like a bulbous, rolling bubble). She drove out of Noe Valley avoiding the BMW 3 Series wagons and sedans, the Passats, the Land Rovers, and the new Noe Valley mothers with their large, three-wheel-bike-style kiddie strollers created for jogging. She drove out north along Castro, turned onto Divisadero, and finally ended up in Presidio Heights with its large, shingled homes and sweeping views of the bay. She dropped the boys off at soccer in the Presidio and drove back to her home for a day of cooking, light cleaning, yoga, and minor appointments. The boys both had play dates after soccer at other kids' homes. This left her with the kind of time that allowed her to think—and here, she had more time to think than she perhaps should have been allowed.

She thought of her life. What she hated about it and what she appreciated. How luxury had been overrated and how luxury was not the issue, per se. She also thought of her children. How she had lost her connection with them so soon after they had come out of the womb. She thought of all this and she thought of the big question of how to change her predicament. Perhaps running away was too extreme, but leaving, just for a while; that might be good.

No packing. No, she would just rush away in the waning sun. She deserved so much more, she knew. She wished she could live away from San Francisco and Noe Valley and clogs and skirts that blew every which way in the wind and got wet in the rain. She wanted to escape cargo pants and vintage-style vests. She wanted to escape the Makhams, the Liebermans, the Fitzpatricks, the Langleys, the Edelkinds, and the Smiths. She needed to escape them all really. She wished to continue on with dance, but, for now, she would drive north.

She had made up her mind.

*   *   *

Barbara had decided that she was leaving for a while. Where to, she did not know. All Barbara knew was that she deserved better— she was certain of this. She deserved a loving husband and grateful kids at least. With these thoughts in her mind, she found herself in her Volvo, stealing away in the night.

Noe Valley's lights were still on. She was swooping around the hills in the hefty wagon. What a cruel existence. She drove a station wagon just as her own mother did, and, really, she decided, the station wagon was the basis for all comparisons that could be made between her mother and herself. Despite being similar in appearance and utility to her mother's wood-paneled Ford Country Squire, Barbara's station wagon handled itself better and had a certain level of ease and luxury in its design that her mother's car simply did not have. A similar difference extended across their own lives. Both occupied the trappings of motherhood, though, unlike her mother, Barb was rarely stuck behind a vacuum or mop. Unlike her also-unhappy mother, Barbara, however, did many things for herself, and though she was almost indulgent, her plight felt the same as her mother's. They were both stuck, really. It began to rain heavy, loud drops on the windshield. Compact droplets of water spread across the windshield.

Few people were on the street. She was so safe, so careful. All people did was take from her; she knew that this was unfair. The sun had set a while ago and she was really leaving. Ahead, past the Pottery Barn and past Market Street she saw darkness. The lights were out in the shops for the second day in a row. The streetlights were out as well. She continued on.

She went ahead, knowing she had the right of way. She gripped the leather-wrapped steering wheel. She plowed forward with few cars in her way. Surrounded by darkness, she was lonely. She had needs that weren't being fulfilled. That was why she chose to leave. She sped up to thirty, then forty miles per hour. She looked at the street around her—chaos. Homes were dark, the stars were highly visible, and a few failing generators unsuccessfully putted along, trying to power the streetlights above.

She sloshed through puddles and felt exhilarated. She swerved, looked at the soft glow of the moon on the Volvo emblem at the center of her steering wheel. As she sped along, some form became visible on the dark street. She was delirious with joy—her liberation, she felt, had arrived. She would return home as a new woman. As she thought all of this, zooming at fifty-five miles per hour in the rain, she killed a woman.

The brakes screeched, of course. She skidded in the rain and slid into a parked car, setting off its alarm. Lying across her smashed windshield was a poor immigrant, a nanny, a Hispanic whose name she'd later learn was Rosa Valdez. She was not old, thirty-one. She had been heavy, though. She smashed the windshield so Barbara could hardly see out. The right wiper had been destroyed. The other wiper continued on, batting at her head. It went up, then back down. It hit her head six times before Barbara turned it off. On the darkened street, she sat with Rosa for a moment—in her car with Rosa's body sprawled out on the hood. Blood smeared on the windshield, mixing with the rain. The wiper stopped mid-wipe.

Barbara pressed the little red triangle, turning on her emergency lights and allowing them to blink away. Safety first. She looked out behind her own door on the driver's side to see if anyone was zooming along as she had been just moments ago. Barbara slipped a bit as she heaved the heavy silver door open against the elements. She felt for a pulse—dead. She began to cry; gentle little tears rolled down her delicate cheek. A car drove by, then another. Onstar, the car's onboard personal assistant, called 911, in knowledge that there had been an accident. The airbags were supposed to be deployed, though that failed to occur. Barbara was conflicted between staying with Rosa on the hood and returning to the dry car and calling for an ambulance that would truck her dead body to San Francisco General Hospital. She returned to the car, where an Onstar assistant was speaking to her, asking what they could do for her.

"I've just hit a woman," Barbara said to the operator.

"Have you attended to her?"

Barbara held her face in her hands, "Yes, she's dead."

Onstar replied, "Thank you. An ambulance is on its way, Mrs. Schwartz."

Soon an ambulance came, lights flashing. It rolled Rosa away. Barbara was not blamed for the death (the city, however, could be sued by Mrs. Valdez's family). The impact was low enough and shown to be at the speed limit. (Barbara was so relieved they never discovered her *actual* speed.) Her family treated her as if she had gained insight on life: Noe Valley was not so bad, she decided. Rosa's family had no such realizations, though. They were left lonely in South San Francisco. Barbara visited them once and tried to explain to Rosa Valdez's husband and mother what had happened, but reported back to David that she never really felt as though she had broken through or connected with them.

Surely Barbara felt sorry for the Valdezes. They had suffered a terrible loss because of San Francisco's freak power outage. Barbara knew then that she would never forget the night when she hit the woman in the rain and lived to tell about it.

Voice in the Night

by GALEN SHEARN-NANCE

Age 10, Bel Aire School

"**W**here am I? Oh my god! Where am I?!" I was lost. About five minutes ago, I had departed from civilization. I had left David, Ben, and all my other fellow fifth-graders behind.

The cabin leader had told me not to worry. "Walker Creek Ranch is a safe place," he had lectured. "There is not a chance that you could get lost. It's only as dangerous as a hike in the daytime." Oh, how wrong he had been. I had done *something* wrong, and now I was lost. I was no coward. I would not go back.

"Help!! Help!!" I screamed, as if my life depended on it. Nothing happened. "Help!! Help!!" a voice called out from the darkness. I rushed toward the sound. Suddenly, I felt my foot stick on a branch. I flew forward into a pothole. I felt a sharp stinging pain and blood dripped slowly onto my face. Darn echoes, I thought to myself. How could I be so stupid as to think that my echo could be someone's voice? I tried to climb out, but the dirt just caved in on me and I found myself buried under five feet of dirt and rocks. And worms, yes, definitely worms. I hated worms. Ickly, stickly worms. They were beginning to crawl over me. Their cold, sticky bodies squirmed and wriggled. Then I felt a sharp pinch, from a beetle maybe, and in my pain my strength seemed to be multiplied by ten. I heaved the rocks and dirt (and worms) off of me. In seconds I had scrambled out of the hole and was dusting myself off.

I wandered for minutes and soon found a large forest looming in front of me. I thought to myself that maybe if I didn't get back to camp in time, the president would send the reserves to get me. I prepared myself to go into the forest. Suddenly, a voice boomed out of the infinite blackness. "Galen," it said. "Is that you?"

"Who's there?" I called out.

"It's me, David." Just these words cheered me greatly. I walked toward the voice: up a cliff, over a stream. At last I reached my friend.

"I wasn't scared, not one bit," I lied. David laughed.

"Sure? I was scared to death. I thought you were a gangster."

"Err... well, I guess I was a little scared." At last we reached the cabin leaders. They took us back to camp, and we went to sleep. Although I loved the night hike, I have nightmares every time I think about it.

The Three Goddesses

by CARSON EVERETT

Age 16, Lowell High School

The word on the street is that Dracula is going to destroy the prom at Bucharest High School. Three goddesses, Marltist, Sulenia, and Colteniaist, want to go to Bucharest, Romania, on a mission to save kids from Dracula. They have decided to save the children in the world from devils. They want to make sure innocence is always protected. In the year 2032 B.C., the triplet goddesses were born in a remote city of Romania. It is now May 27, 1934, and they are 3,966 years old. Colteniaist, the Goddess of War, who has red curly hair and green eyes, is the youngest sister. Marltist, the Goddess of Nature, is the Nordic-looking blonde middle child of the family, and Sulenia, the Goddess of Love, who has brown hair and brown eyes, is the eldest. Colteniaist changes her name to Cordelia so people will not mistake her for some colt. Sulenia changes her name to Sarah so people can pronounce her name correctly. Marltist changes her name to Marlene so she sounds cool like Marlene Dietrich.

The Three Goddesses go to a dress store to buy dresses for the prom. Their real interests are masculine, like fixing hydraulics on airplanes, and they like to wear overalls. The men that see them wearing what they like might be scared of them, so they wear fancy dresses to hide their awesome power. Cordelia picks out a green silk dress that sparkles like foliage on a tree. Marlene picks out a black sequin dress that shimmers like the bay at night. Sarah picks out a red satin dress that shines like a fiery sunset. Although they shop at the dress store, they have to alter the dresses themselves, which makes them a little late. The three sisters get on a Bucharest-bound train.

Cordelia says, "I can't wait to get there; I have only heard of this thing called *The Prom.*"

Sarah says mockingly, "I totally want a date for the prom."

"*Whatever,* I can't wait to get on the dance floor and dance with the boys. Dancing to jazz all night. I can't wait to listen to songs sung by Billie Holiday," sighs Marlene.

Sarah says on the train so she can make the time fly by, "This reminds me of when I went to America on a frigate in 1778. Unfortunately, a revolutionary war was going on. As the ship arrived in the harbor, I saw a man that I thought was swell. When I got on the dock, he told me his name was James Bergen, and he was very friendly to me. The ultimate thing that made James different from others of his time is that he thought women were equal to men. He also was a loving person.

"The Elders, the people who guide us and enforce our Sacred Laws, didn't want me to fall in love with him, but I did. Of course, I knew that it was against the Sacred Laws of Goddesses to marry mortals. I feared for his life. If he loved me and got married to me his life would be in danger constantly. I knew that James would have died from the constant hoards of demons that attack us. I said, 'I'm sorry, dear, but I need some space.' We were good friends from that point on. I was a very good friend, and I nursed him back to health when he was injured from the war. One time, I tripped on my horrible shoes and James caught me. I noticed he was totally crushing on me. I didn't tell him I was a goddess because he might have feared that I could harm him.

"I went to a ball thrown in James' honor in Philadelphia. The

826 QUARTERLY • SUMMER 2004

snake-like British spies were telling the British Army where the American officers were. The British planned to capture James, which I knew from a vision, and from an English source who didn't like the British, but unfortunately I couldn't interfere with the war since it might affect my future. Interfering with mortal matters is against our Sacred Law unless there is a worldwide war. There was a sudden British invasion in the ball, and James was dragged out of the door to the town square where a British officer had a rope to hang him. The Fates were kind to him: Abigail Kingly, a witch and a plantation owner from Atlanta, Georgia, was in the town square at that very moment. Abigail didn't have to follow Goddess Rules. She was a colonist who was an English citizen. She couldn't stand the Parliament, so she defected. Abigail saved him because she wanted to annoy the British Parliament.

"I watched in horror as the British prepared to hang poor James. Right as the British opened the trapdoor, Abigail levitated him away from the rope so he could escape. The British and everybody there were shocked to see this phenomenon. The British soldiers tried to get him down by shooting at him, but they couldn't get him at all because the levitation binding was so strong. When James landed, too far from the British for them to shoot at him, he set eyes on a girl from New Hampshire named Ferisa Johnson. I was crushed that the boy was falling in love with that girl. But I got over it, although I felt that James was still in love with me.

"In 1781, when Cornwallis surrendered to the Americans, James married Ferisa. I did go to the nice wedding, and their wedding reception. Ferisa looked astonishing at both functions, and I was not the center of attention. James Bergen came towards me. I was in a blue silk dress and I had a bustle which I hated wearing. James told me he had to talk to me before he left with his new wife. He told me a dark secret he didn't want his wife to know. He told me he had a crush on me. I went back on a frigate bound for home, so I wouldn't destroy his wonderful marriage. I felt fine about James being in love with Ferisa, since I felt like I did my job as the Goddess of Love.

I let him fall in love with whomever he wanted." Sarah stops talking and begins to fidget with her brown hair.

The train is very dirty because someone did not clean it well. There are crumbs all over the dinner cabin, and there is an oil slick on the train track. Because the train is so dirty, Marlene looks at her Nordic hair, thinking the nasty dinner car befouled her. Cordelia files her nails because the room befouled her with dirt.

The goddesses, unfortunately, are late for the prom. The prom is continuing without Sarah, Marlene, and Cordelia. Most people are asleep on the ride, but the goddesses are still awake. The train arrives in Bucharest at exactly 10:30 p.m. and the girls run to the prom. Marlene is the first among her sisters to get to the door, but she walks in elegantly. The prom is going to be a bust in a minute. Dracula comes through the door. The dancing pauses, and everybody panics.

Dracula yells, "I will eat everyone so there is no escape. I want to suck your blood, bleh! I will end everybody's lives."

Cordelia says, "Hold the phone. You mean to tell me you are going to damage these kids' lives? You drink people's blood, which, by the way, is disgusting. I remember you actually ruined my fingernails. When I looked at that obnoxious face of yours it was so ugly, my nails were cracked in 1674. That year was so embarrassing for me."

Dracula says dismissively, "Be quiet. That didn't happen, did it?"

Sarah replies patiently to Dracula's dismissive way, "Well, I remember you, too, Dracula. You destroyed a lot of people's lives, which annoyed me, especially when I had split ends because I had to go to hell to complain. Satan was there and I had to talk to him."

Marlene says, "You are so ugly. I would have to leave the room if I had to look at your ugly face. I've seen ugly, but, man, you're ugly and stinky and you have no sense of fashion."

Sarah says, "Totally. Dracula, you are so ugly that you are alone, sucking people's blood, just to get human contact."

Dracula says coldly, "*Whatever*, girls."

Marlene decides to put on the poisonous apricot nail polish that Dracula can't stand. Because the Three Goddesses have created it, it causes Dracula to go crazy and he pulls his hair. The apricot fragrance makes Dracula flee the scene. The dance goes on, and most of the kids have already forgotten about what happened. The boys, who don't know Cordelia, Marlene, or Sarah at all, try to ask them to dance. The boys expect to fail because they think the law of physics is that hot gals don't dance with nerdy boys.

The school's prom is fun for a while, but then a problem occurs. In a split second an alarm telepathically reaches Sarah. The alarm is a screech that indicates an invader's presence in their heavenly home. Sarah takes Marlene by the hand, and they levitate to the invader. Then an evil clan of demons named Sanola led by Cronolia, who is a devil, crashes the prom because they know Cordelia is alone.

Cronolia says, "We will destroy everybody's lives in here, so there is no need for panic—got it?"

Cordelia says, "*Whatever.* I know you from a war that happened in 1342. You never could admit that I was better than you, so then you, like, purposefully destroyed my nails in a battle. I was upset— not just because you destroyed my nails—but because you had the gall to destroy my nails *after you lost.*"

Cronolia roars back, "I will get you for your annoying, pure goodness."

Cordelia mockingly replies to Cronolia's roaring by saying, "I see, just send me a Grim Reaper when you're ready to stop my goodness. You can charge it to my credit card bill." Cronolia storms off and bumps into a student.

The tide of a war between angels and devils may come, Cordelia thinks to herself. Cordelia is upset at Cronolia and they are always at each other's throat. Cordelia gets annoyed at arguing with Cronolia, so she goes to obtain a hot boy to dance with. She dances with a boy from America. Cordelia wants to get some fresh air, so she leaves the boy on the dance floor and sits in front of the

Bucharest High School in her lounge chair. Cronolia, from behind a tree, throws a piece of chocolate doughnut at Cordelia. She knows that since the doughnut is sweet, Cordelia will eat it and get totally fat. Cordelia sees the chocolate doughnut on the ground and swoops down to eat it like a falcon would. The doughnut is savory for her. Suddenly, Cronolia sees Sarah and Marlene are near and leaves the vicinity.

Cordelia sees her sisters, Marlene and Sarah, coming down after being in heaven. The heavens are boring today since the alarm was a mistake; a bird had come into their house. They go back to Cordelia, a little grumpy about having missed some of the prom.

"Today has been such an interesting day," says Sarah sarcastically. "You are not taking my advice and using love instead of your usual bullying and warlike tactics."

Marlene says, "She is right. Warlike tactics are natural for you but not right, not all the time."

Cordelia says, "I'm not in high school anymore. Just because I had a reputation for hitting and busting bullies, doesn't mean I do that now."

Cordelia, Sarah, and Marlene are outside when the prom ends. Marlene and Sarah made fools of themselves by leaving the dance when the bird invaded their house. Cordelia sees everybody smiling after the evil had been forced out of the prom. Cordelia is happy to have had fun at the prom.

All the students say, "Great dance! I want to go to another prom just like it."

Marlene in her black sequin dress says, "Too bad I missed the party. I wish I could have seen more of the prom and not have had to go home."

Sarah in her fiery red satin dress says to Cordelia, "At least you were enough of a hero to stay at the prom."

Cordelia in her green silk dress says, "I'm a hero who is ready to go home."

When all the students have left, Cordelia, Sarah, and Marlene levitate to their heavenly home. They comb their hair after the prom. Cordelia puts on strong jasmine perfume to celebrate the defeat of Cronolia. Cronolia was always mean to her and evil to innocent children.

Marlene asks, "What would you like to do, Cordelia, after having defeated Cronolia?"

Cordelia answers, "Nothing. Just be with you guys."

Sarah replies, "Good answer. We want you to be with us as well."

Sarah doesn't talk while fixing her brown hair. There are no battles about to come up so Cordelia, Sarah, and Marlene relax in their house but do housework. Cordelia in her green silk dress and blue four-inch high heels cleans the floors. Marlene, in her black sequin dress and green three-inch high heels, cuts the weeds. Sarah, in her red satin dress and green four-inch high heels, makes the bed. They enjoy cleaning their heavenly home after defeating clueless and tacky demons that have no fashion sense.

Independence
in a Male-Dominated Society

by SARAH KONANE LUM

Age 14, Berkeley High School

No one dared to defy my father; it was an unwritten rule like my daily "confessional" with him. I'd blurt out my day's events; I was a soldier responding to my lieutenant. He'd sit in silence, his back erect, face blank, as he leisurely sipped his pure black coffee (never did he desire sugar or cream). He was sure to let his facial expressions run to hyperbole as he smacked his lips together in satisfaction. Sometimes he'd nod and listen, staring into my honey-colored eyes, light as the caramel squares that hung from yarn in our replica of a 1960s kitchen. Other times he'd completely ignore me, eventually waving me off to my room.

My mother was a housewife, not only serving him, but also balancing two jobs. She'd work from six in the morning 'til four in the afternoon, providing service to Albany High School parents. It was ordinary for her to come home exhausted by the enraged parents that had poured their financial problems onto her like coins from a tip jar. Sometimes I'd offer to massage her feet, allowing her a few minutes of heavenly sleep, pending my father's demand for dinner upon waking from his afternoon nap.

My mother stood short as a Japanese woman, at five foot one.

She grew up speaking Cantonese, Mandarin, and Japanese, and developed a sharp tongue that could cut your soul like a pair of scissors. However, she had a heart so soft that even Franklin Roosevelt would've spared Japan had he met her. Her shoulder-length hair, showing arrogant silver strands through thick black, ran through your fingers like icing on a cake. I never saw her in anything but cashmere, except for the occasional corduroys which were tightly fitted to her once-slender figure.

Full of Japanese customs, my mother ran our house with strict rules unless my father intervened; she was inferior to him. My father believed in "the man taking care of the house" and paid each and every one of our bills. He trusted his philosophy so greatly that he'd argue for days with anyone who disagreed. I depended on my parents equally for support, although I leaned more toward my mom, knowing she was the more compassionate of the two.

My father was an upstanding man, a successful Lum—all his mother could wish for, and all his father could expect. Had he not owned two cars (expensive SUVs at that), a house in the high-class neighborhood of Russian Hill, and borne two beautiful children, my grandfather by no means would have said a peep to him.

My father would stroll through our narrow hallways at midnight, his oversized thirteen-inch feet causing the wooden floors to creak as he slowly inched by like a wildcat on the prowl. The noise made me tingle under my silk-satin bedsheets, but I'd fall asleep soundly to the creaking sound of the floorboards.

Our day started off like any other Sunday. I awoke to my alarm clock beeping noisily at 8 a.m. Hoping my father hadn't awakened, I dressed in silence, peering over at my sister, sure that she was sound asleep. Amy was my role model, the big sister I could count on when I was grumpy with my period and on days when I was pained by the heartbreak of boyfriends. She was my heroine although I would never openly admit it; but even the best of heroes like to sleep in late on Sunday afternoons. I tucked her into her blankets (she usually kicked them off while sleeping) and silently crawled out to the dining room.

To my dismay, as on any other Sunday, my father had rummaged through the Sunday newspaper before I had the chance. The newspaper was folded messily, thrown around our antique, early 1900s oak table. I sighed as I stared down at the blotched coffee stain he had left on the sports section that showcased my sister guarding the legendary, San Diego State-destined Latisha Williams. Grimacing at what my father had done, I hunted for the comic section, eager to read the adventures of *Baby Blues*. Sure enough, Boe found herself in deep trouble for trying to steal her brother's cookie straight from his hands.

I attempted to scramble eggs, which burnt as dark as coal and tasted worse. I had forgotten about the rice, which was no longer steamy or white. Instead, it was muddy brown, like the barren streets in Kagoshima. I had left the heat on by accident while I was doing my weekly cleaning of the entire house (my father believed a clean house represented a "clean" family). Violently slamming the lid shut, I let out a whimper, a little cry in the empty kitchen, angry that I couldn't cook a simple meal. Even the cracked brown tiles seemed to stare mockingly at me. Even the happy pictures of my family vacationing in Paris looked like no more than an attempt at a normal family. I unstrapped my sunshine-printed apron and hurried out of the house, leaving my tears behind.

Jogging relaxed me. I ran around our short cement paved blocks, desperately trying to forget the disordered state I had left the kitchen in. "Amy must still be sleeping," I thought to myself as I rounded the block. "Ha ha ha… that girl never wakes up on a Sunday, not unless you pry her out with a crowbar."

I untied my beaten, grey New Balances as I entered our front door, allowing it to shut with great force. The wind was picking up. "Dirty floor, dirty behavior," my mom would tell me every time I accidentally forgot to take off my shoes before entering the house.

I heard a rumbling noise as I opened the front door. Not sure of what it was, I thought, "Has Dad caught the mouse?" I made my way to the kitchen, where only piles of filthy dishes waited. After all, he had been trying to catch that mouse for days; it had bitten into his brand new pair of North Face hiking boots. "No, he's not here, but I hear his voice. Where is he?"

Unexpectedly, I heard Amy shouting so desperately for help that I had a flashback of the many street children I had seen in Thailand who cried in pain as they starved to their deaths. "Amy!" I was nervous. My father wasn't known in our family as the peacekeeper. In fact, we all knew him as quite the opposite. He had a social mask and a family mask. He'd bare all his chaos within the secret comforts of our house, but he would hide everything behind a perfect "Hollywood smile" when there was someone of importance present.

"Amy," I thought, "what did you do this time? Why are you always getting into trouble? You're a good person Amy, why do you start this with him? It can only lead to trouble, why don't you know that by now?"

I turned the knob of the placid, white door on which Amy and I had randomly placed sunflower stickers. I found my father atop my sister, strangling her with his enormously bulging, muscular arms, his veins popping as his grip tightened. His grip was solid, his arms locked, forcing her to his mercy. He had neither pity nor conscience, for now he was spitting in Amy's mouth, waiting for her to swallow. My mother hovered over him, demanding that he move as she pulled and pried at his concrete 215-pound body. Weary, she eventually collapsed on the bed weeping, deciding she had failed. "Get off! I'm going to call the cops! Get off of her, Dad!" *Dad* seemed such an unfit word I had to grit my teeth.

"Then call the damned cops; they won't do anything! I'm a law-abiding citizen, dammit!" He continued to choke her, the once tanned complexion of her face slowly turning ghostly white. Her eyes boggled passionately; I could barely see a hint of brown.

Her legs shook ferociously as she tried to pry his arms away from her swollen neck, purple from the grasp he continued to hold.

"Don't you ever cuss at me again, Amy, or I'll kill you!" His words rang in my ears, his low monotonous voice barreling over Luther Vandross, who was ironically singing "Dance With My Father" on the radio.

Amy nodded her head with all the energy she could muster; he had been on top of her for minutes, allowing her only a few breaths of air. Slowly, after he was sure she had agreed, he lifted himself off, brushed the ironed shirt my mom had dry-cleaned the day before, and, as if nothing had happened, walked out.

I looked down at Amy as she clenched her throat, and gasped rapidly and repeatedly. She appeared to be vacantly amused by the black mosquito that inched across the cracked-paint ceiling. The room was stuffy; the smell of my dad's dry-cleaned clothes hung in the still air. I went over to the closest window and let in the sweet aroma of freshly cut grass from the lavish, pruned garden that my mom spent hours dwelling in each day.

I stared out at my father, watching him pace back and forth on the pavement as if deep in thought. He didn't appear as confident as he usually did, and his stride of achievement was gone.

Collapsed in exasperation, I had a sudden epiphany: the innocence of childhood had finally left me. I was no longer a mere child of eleven; no more could I be like all the other eleven-year-olds at my school, daydreaming of my next boyfriend or basketball game. It was my duty to my mom and Amy to rise above my father, to be the ultimate success of the family that both could see as a true role model. I have felt this duty so strongly that, to this day, he has never walked over me (or my family) again.

Outsider

by GRAHAM ROGERS
Age 14, Berkeley High School

I always feel like I'm on the outside,
a mote of silence in a screaming horde
afraid of the hellish train of society to ride,
one foot on the platform and one on board.

Everyone else knows "the word on the street,"
but I'm the only one who doesn't understand.
Everyone else has their own price to meet,
but I can't seem to meet society's demand.

So I have carved out my own little niche
where my cares and worries don't spread me
    so thin.
But heaven is hell, its beauty bewitched:
there are vultures without and demons within.

But there also are angels, outcasts like me.
It's because of them that I remain free.

Going Home

by KIRA DEUTCH

Age 16, Jewish Community High School of the Bay

The sun moons the world between
   the trees,
a blinding white
like kids on mischief night
trying to get someone to see.
I look away from the window
and wait for the train to go underground
so the light show can start.
Yellow, blue, white lights shoot
past the subway window
like comets,
all heading to where I came from.
The train surfaces and the sun flirts again,
a piercing pain I've felt before,
coquettish and indiscriminate.
I hate its lusty warmth,
its dangerous promiscuity,
shining for everyone.

The Poem

by JOSEPH COTSIRILOS
Age 12, Home-schooled

The snowflakes came down in sheets on the little cottage that was almost buried in snow. It was a very small cottage; the word shack would be a better term for it. It was one of those houses that little children playing ball would whisper about what they thought was inside; in other words, it wasn't all that attractive. And maybe the children were right, for it actually wasn't all that fancy. Only a single candle along with a bed, a small desk, a stove, a sink, and a very out of tune piano were the contents. There was also something that nobody knew was there: a tall, rather young man with bandages around one of his fingers. Nobody quite knew him; nobody even knew his name. The only one who knew his name was the man who owned the cottage; it was Daniel.

Daniel mostly stayed inside his house, but occasionally he could be seen in the main plaza, looking at the plants. He was pleasant to people but he never talked much; one could say he was reserved. But reserved in that case would be the perfect antonym. For although Daniel might have seemed reserved in his goings about town, he was completely different when it came to a pen and paper. Usually he spent his time writing poetry in his cottage.

The very-out-of-tune piano he had was nothing he enjoyed

110

very much. He once thought of selling it to pay off his pile of bills, but when one of the legs broke, the only thing Daniel could see was another piece of paper in his face saying he owed even more. "How ignorant of them!" Daniel exclaimed after he received the bill and closed the door. "They should make their pianos more suitable for the normal person." After hearing that sentence, the reader might think that he was irritable, but he was not. He had a mighty good time looking at the nice bouquets of flowers in the plaza and had many pleasant little thoughts.

One of the reasons he wasn't in town very much is that it was a three-mile hike across the woods he lived in. Daniel liked looking at gardens but didn't like to go out much. Now that I think about it, the word reserved might have been a good word to describe him.

Daniel flipped the thin metal pan he used for cooking into his hand. After setting the burner on his stove for some inhuman number of degrees, he threw in some cheese, meat, and eggs making a very odd tasting omelet. Maybe that was another one of the reasons people didn't like to be around him; he wasn't very tidy. He left half of the sizzling mix of eggs and other things on the burner and brought the plate he had to his desk where he began to eat.

Most people would have put their finished plates in a pile to be washed, but Daniel just put his on the floor with the other pile of unclean things. Daniel took out his pen and watched the snowflakes drift down through the various cracks along the walls, door, windows, and occasionally the ceiling. He watched how one speck of ice drifted and spun in the air; it almost looked like a little kingdom. Without hesitation, he began to write:

> The snowflake drifts with unseen passion and raw emotions.
> It is graceful yet it is harsh,
> Cutting through the air like a hawk in the wind, sharp talons
>   piercing the cry of the sky.

He then stopped and put down his quill only to knock over the inkwell that was on the corner of his desk. The ink stained the floor and everything that was in arm's reach of it. Daniel cursed angrily and watched it go through the holes in the floor and into the snow. Daniel stopped for a second and picked up his quill and tried to write again.

"Damn this quill," Daniel said, after realizing there was not much ink left to write with.

Daniel paused and then got up from his chair. He blew out the candle and soon left cursing to himself. Being a man who got barely any exercise, Daniel thought it would be nice just to go for a walk. As it was, there was nothing else he could do.

Many people would take pleasure in looking at the strong and tall frost-covered trees, but with such cruel coldness one could only hope to last through the day. Many children would have climbed the trees and would have snowball fights, but not at this time of day, for it was late, and England needed to rest. Daniel also didn't like the idea of walking around dressed in informal clothes when there were fine women dressed in large dresses. But Daniel did not care much, as he walked only through the woods and not in town.

The only person whom he would care to see was the lady with a nice little house not far from his; she was a nice lady and Daniel was very fond of her. Her name was Elizabeth. Daniel stopped and thought that it might be nice to knock on her door for a cup of tea. No sooner had he finished his thought when he came to the door; three hard knocks followed.

The door opened and a beautiful lady with long hair draping over her shoulders stood there.

"Why Daniel, hello. Come on in. You must be cold."

"Oh, why thank you, Elizabeth, I'll do just that."

Daniel walked into Elizabeth's nice house and sat himself down on a velvet couch. He soon realized that he was not the only one on the couch. A fine black cat stood next to him, purring and rubbing its head into his elbow.

Elizabeth's house was a very nice one—very homey. The rooms were dressed up with many tall candles. The house was well lit. Daniel most loved the tapestries on the walls. He enjoyed looking at them while sitting in front of a nice fireplace that was burning with pride. It was the type of home that a humble man would dream of having. Elizabeth sat down in a lounge chair that was across from Daniel, her hair swinging in the light of the candles. Daniel watched her sit down and saw how her hair reflected the light and how it glistened. Daniel longed to feel her hair and feel the smooth silk-like texture.

Elizabeth spoke, "So Daniel, what is it you came for?"

Daniel paused and then after thinking for a while he replied, "I was wondering if you had a spare inkwell I could borrow."

Elizabeth smiled and brushed her long black hair aside before saying, "What is it you need the inkwell for, to write with?"

"I would like it to, Elizabeth! Of course I would need it to write with!"

Elizabeth laughed a little and poured him a cup of tea. She set the cup and the teapot on the small glass table that separated them. The tea had a nice smell to it; it smelled of roses but had something else in it that caught Daniel's attention. Elizabeth poured the steaming tea into the china cups with flowers on them. Daniel noticed that they were painted with some type of oil paint, for the paint coating was thick.

Elizabeth sat down once again and said, "I think I have a spare inkwell. Hold on one second."

She got up and walked into another room. Daniel sat on the couch and petted the cat that was sitting in his arms purring. Daniel smiled and ran his hand through the soft fur of the cat. He always liked cats; he wanted to have one but he never got around to it. He looked at the wonderful decorations that were inside the house and tried to compare them to his own. Daniel scoffed a little realizing that they were both very different.

"There is a line that separates us," Daniel said, petting the black cat. "It is a line that, even so far away, I wish to cross someday."

"What did you say, Daniel?"

Daniel looked up and saw Elizabeth coming out of the other room holding something in her hand. She had a look on her face as though she had misheard something.

"Oh nothing," Daniel replied as the cat hopped down from his lap and made his way over to the bowl of milk that was in another room.

Elizabeth sat down again and put the thing that was in her hand on the table. She unwrapped it and gave it to Daniel; it was a spare inkwell with very top quality ink. Daniel stared at it surprised, and then opened his mouth to say something, but a soft hand met his and his mouth closed. The hand belonged to Elizabeth, who helped him up from the couch and said, "Thank you very much for coming."

"You are very welcome," Daniel said and then kissed her hand.

The two of them parted and Daniel walked back to his cottage and sat back down at his desk. He saw things as he had left them that day: an unfinished omelet on the stove, the ink stains on the floor, and, most of all, the beginning of his new poem. Daniel picked up his quill, dipped it in the ink and began to write again. He first started by reading what he had already written:

The snowflake drifts with unseen passion and raw emotions.
It is graceful yet it is harsh,
Cutting through the air like a hawk in the wind, sharp talons
*   piercing the cry of the sky.*

Daniel smiled and picked up his quill and twirled it. The ink sped across the fine piece of parchment that lay on his desk. He wrote this:

She is graceful as she rests on the surface of the water like
*   a feather,*

Her smooth skin that is cold as ice but comforting.
The snowflake is a beautiful piece of art
That was made by the paintbrush that belonged to some
splendid artist somewhere—
An artist I would most like to meet.

Daniel stopped and put his quill aside. He rested his head on his hand and then got up. He then read all of the poem aloud:

The snowflake drifts with unseen passion and raw emotions.
It is graceful yet it is harsh
Cutting through the air like a hawk in the wind, sharp talons
piercing the cry of the sky.
She is graceful as she rests on the surface of the water like
a feather,
Her smooth skin that is cold as ice but comforting.
The snowflake is a beautiful piece of art
That was made by the paintbrush that belonged to some
splendid artist somewhere,
An artist I would most like to meet.

Daniel smiled and put the paper in a drawer in his desk. He let it rest there with many other poems that reflected his feelings at various points in time. Daniel got into bed and began to sleep. His eyes jolted open when he heard a scratching on his door. Daniel tiredly opened the door and found a brown kitten meowing. Daniel looked into its soft hazel eyes and picked it up and brought it into his house. He shut the door and then got a towel. With the towel he began to dry the kitten off. He then got a bowl and filled it with water. After doing so he got some meat and placed it on a plate and watched the kitten eat hungrily.

Daniel began to tidy up his cottage a bit. It was something he didn't do very much, but he decided that he would be much happier if his house was clean. He began with the omelet, then he cleaned off the pots and pans. This went on quite some time. Soon, the little cottage was clean. Daniel smiled, sat on his bed and looked at the house. It was a much happier place to live in. The kitten hopped on his lap and for that happy night, they slept together. It had been a very good day for the both of them.

[*Editors' note: This first chapter of* The Forsaken Veteran *represents the beginning of what we hope will become a complete novel.*]

The Forsaken Veteran

by ALEX KIVELSTADT

Age 16, The Urban School of San Francisco

Chapter One

The air was heavy, weighing him down. The added effect that it was ice-cold only made it even more uncomfortable. It reeked of death and decay, the crumbling ruins of an old world giving way to the new. The area was nothing but rubble and other debris. Nothing in this forsaken wilderness ever looked beautiful and had not for many years. The sky was dark, like it always was, even in the middle of the day. The only other visible objects in the sky besides the faint sun were dark venomous clouds, which were avoided by all. Shadows moved along the ground.

The air made his skin crawl. He felt as if it were eating away at his body through his thick jacket and pants. He took a breath through his mask and he felt stale air push up into his nostrils. He hadn't been able to remove his mask outside the dome since he was born. His goggles fogged up as he exhaled, temporarily blocking his view of the desolate landscape.

He inhaled and exhaled one more time, this time motioning with his hand for the rest of his group to move forward. This was no ordinary group wandering through the ruins; these were warriors. Though none were past the age of twenty, they were all sea-soned veterans who could defend themselves. The man looked around at the faces following him, and he couldn't help but feel sorry for what was happening. Mere children made to fight. The light that normally shone in their eyes had long since been replaced with the cold sheen of killers.

The gun in his hands felt cold, the metal constantly cooled by the frigid air. He knelt by a pile of ash and used his brown gloves to inspect it. He felt the dry texture through the material, felt it fall between his fingers like sand. A big one was near, and his small squad of ten might have some trouble handling this one. He motioned for them to take up positions and turned away from them.

He stood, finally stretching his tall frame. He was a little over six feet, quite a big person for the time. He was broad-shouldered and he wore a grey jacket and grey pants. His company emblem was on his right shoulder: the image of a dragon with a sword in its claws, which reminded all who saw him that he was the leader of the Slayers, the best tracking team in the area.

His brown boots were filthy, along with the rest of his uniform, but he was used to it by now. He trudged through the ash and dirt without concern, meaning to draw out the creature they were seeking. He slung his gun over his back, the silver catching in the light of the dim sun, casting a dull flare behind him. As he walked forward, he put his left hand on the scabbard at his hip, and with his right hand drew out his sword.

The sword also caught the faint sunlight, but in a different way. The sun tried to push itself onto the blade, but was instead devoured by it. Pure black, the sword's obsidian blade absorbed all light as if it were a black hole. In his left hand he drew out his pistol, this combination his style of choice.

His squad knew that he meant business now and watched with renewed vigor as their captain walked through the debris until he came upon a building that was blocking his way. He looked it up and down, recognizing it as a multileveled garage for vehicles back in the ancient times. He leveled his pistol and shot twice.

The two blasts blew out the supports of the building, causing it to collapse in on itself. The dust plume that followed blanketed everything. This was planned though, as the goggles the captain and his men wore were designed to see through almost all types of sludge and fog.

The captain heard a noise to his left, and he dove forward. He fell into a roll, coming up onto his feet as he heard something land where he had stood a mere second before. He spun, knowing what was behind him. At least twelve feet tall, the creature had four arms, two ending in scythe-like claws, and the other two ending in clawed hands. Its face a mass of teeth and flesh, the creature tensed, prepared.

The beast jumped toward the captain, but the captain saw this, and plunged to his right. As he did, his squad opened fire, their guns blasting dozens of holes in the creature's back and legs. But even with these wounds, the creature turned on the captain and stalked toward him.

As the creature came in, it cocked its scythe-like blades back and slammed them down toward the captain who used his blade to block one while he rolled to the right. The other just scraped his left shoulder, a small red line now visible on his arm beneath the tear in his jacket. The captain missed this, too concentrated on the real problem: he was now stuck between two scythes.

The creature bent forward, its two clawed hands reaching for the captain's face. The captain could smell it through his mask, and he had to clench his teeth to stop from vomiting. He turned his wrist, ready to use his sword, but the creature stopped. It rocked forward for a few seconds, then collapsed to the ground.

The captain looked up to see all guns trained on where the creature had been standing. He grinned behind his mask. He knew that his squad was the best, and this proved it. They had taken down a creature with such precise shooting that it had simply collapsed. The grin was gone, though, as he saw their faces.

"We're going back now," the captain said quickly as he stood and sheathed his sword. "You guys aren't looking so hot, so let's get the hell out of here."

The group was just as silent on the return as on the way out. Something had happened, something awful that he couldn't pinpoint. The captain saw the dome on the horizon, and he let out a long sigh of relief. There was no need for them to fight anymore today, which was good since he wanted them to get over what had disturbed them.

They neared the dome, and two guards immediately recognized them. They quickly talked into the com on the wall, announcing their arrival. The guards motioned for the group to stop; the normal scan was about to commence. The captain watched as the green light washed over them, deep-scanning for the virus.

The two guards watched the results and immediately looked at the captain. One called into the com while the other hoisted his gun to his shoulder. The squad quickly did the same, but the captain motioned for them to stand down.

"I'm sorry, sir," the guard at the com said walking towards him. "We are going to have to take you to get cleaned up. You have been infected by the virus. Come with me."

"Wait a second," the second in command of the Slayers called out while grabbing the coat of the guard and hoisting him off his feet. "What are you talking about our captain getting 'cleaned up'? Don't they have a shot for it?"

"Well, y-yes," the guard replied, shaken. "But the longer we delay, the less the chances of success are."

The second-in-command dropped the man on the ground, about to bash down the door to escort his captain to the medical labs. A hand was placed on his shoulder, though, and he turned to see his captain holding him back.

"I'll be perfectly fine," the captain said while walking past him.

"Vyse, make sure they all get to their rooms in good order. See you guys soon."

"See you, captain," came the response from the entire squad as they saw their captain escorted to the medical labs.

The captain knew this was bad. He had never been infected before, but he had heard the stories of what could happen. A shiver went through his spine as he thought about what he would become if he weren't treated in time. He closed his eyes and exhaled, the footsteps ringing in his head.

The captain watched the dull grey interior pass by as he walked. It was a lifeless hallway, as the whole dome was. Everything seemed dim, even the light of the people's eyes. The captain looked around him as people came to see why someone was being escorted by soldiers.

He smiled to a few, but they seemed to recoil, and this really bothered him. He was one of the most liked soldiers in the dome, yet people seemed to fear him now because of a little scratch. The group passed through one more doorway, and the next hallway was narrow and white.

The guard in front of him was reaching into his pocket, and the captain noticed this with interest. He pulled out a cigarette and lit it, puffing out a cloud of smoke that fell back onto the captain's face. The captain coughed, and smacked the cigarette out of the man's hand.

"What the hell do you think you're doing?" the guard asked while reaching for his gun.

"You'd think that you would want to live as long as possible," the captain said, continuing to walk toward the medical bays. "Those things kill you, moron."

The man sneered and kept walking. The captain grinned to himself, but as if he had been shot, a wave of pain and nausea washed over his body and he fell to his knees. The guard behind him quickly yelled something into his com, but the captain couldn't hear it.

He collapsed to the ground, the strength gone from his arms and legs. He could see people rushing to him, but he suddenly lost his sight as he fell unconscious. The men around him lifted him up onto a stretcher and rushed him into the operating room. This would be cutting it close, and they didn't want to lose such a man as this.

The captain awoke, pain wracking his whole body. He could feel a cool sweat causing chills to race down his spine. He tried to sit up, but leather restraints kept him down. He tried to move his arms and legs, but they were also firmly secured. He looked up, but bright lights shone right into his face, blinding him. He could see that he was in a white circular room with only one door.

He moved his head, panic sweeping through his mind. What happened? Had it been too late to treat the virus? Now were they going to kill him, or worse, experiment on him? As these thoughts raced through his head, he heard the door open to his right and moved his head to see who it was.

A well-groomed man in a white coat entered, his grey hair ragged. He was flanked by two guards, both with their rifles trained on the captain. The man in the white coat stopped, and he looked the captain over.

"Well, Captain Jet," the man began, folding his arms across his chest, "I've got some good news and some bad news. Which one would you like to hear first?"

"Just tell me what the hell happened to me!" Jet yelled as best he could while struggling against his restraints. "And tell me why I am stuck to this table."

Jet was uncomfortable. He didn't like being strapped down to a table where he couldn't do anything. He knew that something was wrong, but he didn't know what it was. He could feel the sweat pouring off his body, soaking the table underneath him.

"Well, we were able to save your life." The man paced back and forth next to Jet's table. "But, we couldn't remove the virus from your body. We only managed to contain it."

"You mean that damn thing is still in my body?" Jet yelled, exasperated. "You better get that thing out of me or I swear I'll—"

"You'll do nothing," the man said curtly, cutting the captain off in mid-sentence. "It's contained, but if we had removed it, it could've kill you. There was no need for the risk."

"Can the virus ever get past the containment you set up?" Jet didn't want to know the answer. He didn't want to know what was going to happen to him. All he wanted to do was get away from these people. But that was impossible, as the straps couldn't be broken by human will.

"We don't know," the man said, turning from the table and walking towards the door. "We have never had to do this before."

With that, the man was gone, and Jet was released by the two soldiers and helped out of the room. Jet was in bad shape; he could feel his body aching. He collapsed from the pain when he was out of the white room, as if something were inside him, tearing him apart.

"Here you are, sir," the guard lay Jet down in his room. "You aren't allowed to leave the dome for one week—is that clear?"

"Yeah, yeah," Jet said, waving his hand weakly in their direction. "Leave me alone."

Jet heard the door close, and with that he closed his eyes. What was going to happen to him? How could he face his men when he could become the very thing they were hunting? Such questions distracted him and numbed him to the pain wracking his entire body as he fell asleep.

No dreams filled his head while he slept, no nightmares or memories. He only saw his thoughts as they drifted through the blackness of his mind. He couldn't remember the last time he had slept this way, but it was a nice change from the nightmares he normally experienced while both asleep and awake.

He awoke to a knock on his door. Bolting upright, he felt waves of nausea course through his body. He fell back onto his bed, his body covered in a cool sweat. He closed his eyes, imagining what his life would have been like if the wars hadn't erupted all over the planet.

"Sir, may I come in?"

"Yes, you may, Vyse," Jet answered slowly as he tried to sit up again in his bed, this time taking his time. "How is the squad holding up?"

As Vyse entered, Jet could immediately tell that they were all worried about him. He knew that he couldn't tell them about his condition, but what could he tell them? It would completely ruin their relationship—better to make something up so that they wouldn't have to worry or know. But he knew he would have to tell Vsye, for he was his best friend.

"They're alright, Captain, but they would be better off knowing that their captain was in good shape." Vyse turned away from his captain. "Unfortunately, we have been told that you are not allowed many visitors and are not allowed to leave for one week. Is this true?"

"It is." Jet stood up from his bed and walked to a window overlooking the center of the dome. "They couldn't get rid of the virus. It is still inside me, but it is contained. The men can't hear about this, understood?"

Vyse turned towards his captain, his best friend, and looked up to see his captain hunched over, both arms across his stomach. Vyse quickly got to his feet, helping the captain to his bed. He looked into the ashen eyes of his friend, and he had to turn away.

"How long do you think you can last against it?" Vyse asked, crossing his arms. "How long do we have before we have to hunt you? Because I can't do it."

"You will do it if you have to," Jet responded coolly, lowering his head. "As for time, they have no idea. They think it may be contained for good, but they aren't sure."

There was silence for a few minutes; the two knew that Jet would last the week at best. They locked stares and Vyse nodded. He left the room, walking towards the mess hall to break the news of the captain to the squad. Not the whole truth, but some of it.

Jet rolled over on his bed, feeling the rough material scratch against his face. He looked out again through the window, but something caught his eye. He saw a hole in the dome, not through the wall, but from the ground. He searched around the ground level for some time before he saw something emerge.

It had two arms, like a human, but it was bent over, its body almost parallel to the ground. It had a tail and claws on its feet and hands. Its head was bulbous, and its mouth was filled with razor-sharp teeth. It was holding some type of gun, and the gun itself seemed to be alive.

"Intruders! Intruders! The dome has been infiltrated!" the loud speaker announced before it started with its instructions. "Every soldier must report to the main courtyard to contain the Horde."

"Crap," was all Jet managed to say as he scrambled for his armor and helmet. He didn't feel well enough to don them, but he had to protect the dome with his life. He managed to get into his uniform, and his helmet followed. His pistol was soon in his left hand, his sword in his right.

As he emerged from the room, he noticed both of the men stationed to guard him were gone. He smirked. *No need to deal with them*, he thought. He made his way down the corridor, his right hand on the wall for support, his breath labored. A few soldiers made their way past him as he hobbled toward the central courtyard.

Once there, his mouth fell open. This wasn't a small breach, but an invasion. Hundreds of soldiers were battling hundreds of the Horde creatures. Adrenaline coursed through the captain's body, and his pain was gone.

He saw his squad holding their own in a main corridor, and he rushed to them, stumbling as he went. Before arriving, though, one of the smaller Horde creatures, a Crawler, got in his way. But it didn't remain long as his pistol found its head, blowing it to pieces.

The smell was revolting, and he again found himself on the verge of vomiting, collapsing to one knee. The nausea enticed him to give in. He held on, though, and charged the rest of the way to his group as they gunned down another wave of Crawlers. When his squad saw him, it was as if they had won the battle. They all cheered. The smiles on their faces quickly faded when they saw the remaining Horde forces turn on them.

The other doors had been sealed, only theirs was open. Hundreds of guardsman had fallen, all in various stages of the virus. Jet cursed, knowing that they had a large amount of killing to do. He looked to Vyse and nodded, leaning against the wall for support as another wave of the virus washed over him, stealing his strength.

"All right, Slayers," Jet started, raising his sword weakly above his head. "Now, let's give 'em hell!"

With that, the real fight began. The Crawlers came in fast, climbing along the walls and on the ground. Behind them stood creatures about ten feet tall, their whole bodies covered in a bone-like armor. They had four arms, two of which held either a barbed whip or a sword. The other two held a gun, the bullets of which seemed to hunger for human flesh. These were the Elites.

Jet saw his friend Monica look hard at the creatures before she hoisted her sniper rifle to her shoulder. She was their marksman, and she would not disappoint them. Next to her, Ken lowered his flamethrower, ready to unleash the flames of hell upon the creatures. Amanda was next. A close combat expert, she wielded two swords. Next to her stood Bill, James, Calria, and Mooruna, all of whom used the standard issue assault rifles. Vyse, like Jet, held a pistol and sword like Jet, and the two stood with Monica to the side. Behind them all stood their most intimidating member, Taurus, named for his immense size and strength. He held a gun normally meant for an emplacement.

The wave of Crawlers never made it within twenty feet of the Slayers, the entire wave cut apart by shot after shot. The Elites came in, the shots from the squad's assault rifles bouncing off their armor like stones. Now, it was Ken's turn as he stepped forward and hosed down the entire group with flames. They heard shrieks and noises that no human could emit. The smell was so potent that Ken fell backwards, his senses overwhelmed.

A few Elites struggled through the flames, their guns firing at the humans. Bill and James were hit, and both fell to the ground. Miniature creatures were devouring Bill's body, while James was lying in a pool of his own blood, his throat pierced. This was about all Jet, Amanda, and Vyse could take as they charged the huge creatures. Jet passed over Monica's body on his charge, her face ashen pale from her loss of consciousness.

"You bastards!" Three humans fell upon the two remaining Elites. One creature with two swords was surrounded by Amanda and Vyse, while the other, wielding whip and sword, faced off with Jet. The three yelled in unison, "For the world and the Slayers!" With that, the fight ensued.

First, Amanda and Vyse circled in opposite directions, trying to split their opponent's attacks or expose its back. It turned to Amanda and slammed both swords down in a long arc. Amanda leapt to the side of both blades, knowing full well that the creature's strength was immense. She rolled to her feet to see Vyse thrust his sword into the kneecap of the Elite's right knee while blasting the other with his pistol.

The creature fell to its knees as Amanda charged in, thrusting both blades into its eyes. The creature shrieked and raised its gun for her stomach. Amanda couldn't dodge it, and she closed her eyes expecting the blow to come. She heard one shot, but she didn't feel any pain.

She looked down to see Vyse's blade in front of the gun, which deflected the blast into the ground just before the creature's body collapsed over it. She helped Vyse to his feet, and turned to see Jet still squared off with his opponent. She was going to move in to help when Jet held his hand up, and she stopped, knowing that it was Jet's fight now.

"You really piss me off, you know that?" Jet exclaimed while twirling his blade in his right hand and grinning despite his pain.

"I'm going to tear you apart for what you did to my friends."

With those last words, Jet charged into the creature, just as its whip went straight for his head. Jet rolled to the left, anticipating the strike, but a shot of pain caused him to collapse to the side. He also foresaw the sword stroke for his head as he rolled backwards and popped to his feet while slashing into the creature's side.

The creature staggered back, but snarled and tried to whip him again. The creature caught Jet's black sword, which was soon popped from his grasp by the brute's strength. Jet cursed with a grin on his face as he blasted the whip out of the creature's hand, both warriors now down to one weapon.

"Well, I think we are even again," Jet laughed at the creature, which only snarled and charged. "Eager to die, aren't we?"

Jet dodged to the left, slamming the butt of his pistol into the creature's hand. He had forgotten about the gun, which was soon pointing at him as he collapsed to his knees again from the pain. Jet could only curse as the creature went to pull the trigger. But fortune seemed to be with Jet, as the creature's head as well as most of its torso exploded.

"Thanks, Taurus. I owe you one," he said while retrieving his sword without turning. "Okay everyone, let's try and help the wounded, and make sure to dispatch the ones that are too far gone so that we don't get any more of these damn things walking around and attacking our backs. Let's move!"

As he turned to look at his squad, he fell to his knees. He could feel his vision swimming before his eyes, and then, as if someone had hit him over the head, Jet fell unconscious to the ground, the blackness consuming him.

He heard noises around him; a constant humming drove him to swing with his right hand, slapping something, driving it back-wards. He heard a curse, and he opened his eyes to see a group of doctors huddled over him, their machines humming away. They looked him up and down; one reached down and performed a test on him with some random instrument.

They were all in white, and it seemed he was back in that damned room with the white walls. He struggled to move, but he had no strength left. He tried to mumble something, but the only sound he made was a garbled gurgling noise. The people around him fell back a few steps, as if something were frightening them. He felt pain course through his body; he had to do something quickly.

"Is he still really alive after that?" Jet heard one of them ask, while others mumbled responses he couldn't hear. "What should we do with him?"

Jet gathered all of his strength, all the concentration and anger welling in his throat, and tried to focus his vocal cords and his mind. He blocked out the doctors and the other people in the room, not wanting to waste energy listening to their drivel.

"Wh-what h-h-happened t-to me?" he managed to ask after several minutes of concentration and pain.

"He talked?" one doctor asked in horror, backing away from Jet. "How could anyone survive this long and retain their humanity?"

"B-because it t-takes more than a l-little v-virus to take me down," Jet coughed out, his body almost spent from the energy needed to say but a few words. "N-now, explain t-to me what i-is going on."

A long moment of silence. No one said anything as they listened to Jet's labored breathing, the raspy noise that followed each of his inhalations. One of the men motioned to the others, and all but one took a step back.

"Well, as you know, you have been infected by the virus," he said slowly, pacing, his hands crossed behind his back. "There was a problem when the Horde attacked us yesterday. The virus inside your body seemed to spread, and, well, we managed to contain it within your body, but it seems that you don't have much time before you will become one of them."

"W-well, that's just peachy," Jet coughed back sarcastically. "So t-tell me, h-how long do I h-have before it's too late?"

A long silence again. Everyone inside the room was still. The silence was broken this time by someone tapping his foot nervously, in a steady pattern.

"To put it blankly," another doctor said as he stepped forward. "We don't know how long you have before this field fails, and when it does, you will become one of... them."

Jet thought how awful it would be to be one of the creatures he hunted. Constantly having the need to feed, yet always being hunted by the very prey you seek. *Oh well*, he thought, as a smile crossed his face, unnerving the doctors in the room. *I'll make the best of it.*

He somehow managed to find the strength to sit up, and he looked each of the doctors over before he looked down, trying to put his thoughts into words. It took him a few moments, and when he looked up again, the doctors all took a step back, seeing the grin splayed across his face.

"This is what's going to happen," Jet said with newfound strength. "I'm going to keep on doing my duties until I die, and there is nothing that you can do about it."

With that, he slid off the table, but when his feet hit the floor, he lost all of his strength again, and he collapsed. The doctors were not coming to help him, paralyzed by the fear that he could already be transforming. One doctor ran out of the room, hurrying towards the city council.

"Captain Jet of the Slayers," a voice said from above Jet when he was able to move again. "By order of the Ruling Council, you are hereby banished from New San Francisco, and by 1400 hours you must be out of this dome on punishment of death."

With that, the two soldiers hoisted Jet up to his feet and carried him to his room. Before reaching their destination, however, Jet's squad stood in the hallway, blocking their progress. With arms crossed and faces set, they didn't budge when ordered to stand down.

"How could you do this to someone like him?" Vyse asked as he balled his fists and stalked towards the two soldiers. "He has served under this military for ten years, and this is how you repay him? By throwing him out when he needs our help?"

"U-under the o-order of the R-ruling C-council," the soldier started, his voice trembling from fright. "Any person or persons who disagrees with this verdict will hereby be exiled from this dome along with the captain. That includes all of you if you try to hinder us anymore."

Vyse snorted, looking from side to side at his comrades, and he turned his attention back to the soldier. He crossed his arms, a smirk coming to his face. He walked a few steps toward the soldier who had been talking, bending down a little to come eye to eye with him.

"Over our dead bodies will you kick the Captain out of here," he said coolly, his tone promising the death of all those who stood in their way. "If you want to kick the captain out, you'll have to kick us out as well. And what would this pathetic dome do without its most elite squad? It wouldn't last too long, would it?"

The soldier backed up a few steps, trying to compose himself. He looked startled. Everyone knew that these warriors were one of the main reasons that this small dome hadn't fallen victim to the ravaging Horde. The soldier cleared his throat, remembering that anyone who went against the edict of the Ruling Council could be punished by death.

"I'm sorry, but you must all leave this dome along with Captain Jet if you don't want to be killed on the spot," the soldier said, visibly shaking from the fear that he would soon find himself dead at the hands of these superb warriors. "If you will excuse me, I must carry this edict to the head of the military so that they can learn of the traitorous acts of their most illustrious unit. You have three hours."

Vyse watched the two soldiers leave after the guards had handed Jet over. He punched the wall with all of his strength. How could the dome turn its back on the very unit that had saved it from destruction dozens of times? No matter now. They had to find a way to get out of the dome before three hours were up or they would be executed.

"Okay," Vyse started, turning to face the rest of the Slayers. "You don't have to come along with the captain and me, but if you do not choose to go, you will be stricken from the ranks of the Slayers. Then, you will probably die at the hands of the Horde once they destroy this complex following our absence. We at least stand a chance against them out there together. So, what will it be?"

THE STORE
at 826 VALENCIA

"Definitely one of the top five pirate stores I've been to recently."
—DAVID BYRNE

What happens at the Store at 826 Valencia? Many have said that upon entering the shop, they get a sensation of déjà vu. Others walk in and feel at once the miracle work of an unseen hand. In fact, our sales of pirate supplies at reasonable prices are one of our major sources of funds. Without our pirate supply sales, we wouldn't be able to pay the rent. It's true! For the edification of this quarterly's readership, here are the particulars of a few of the supplies we sell.

New Items:

Mini Hourglasses
Make your underlings swab the decks at warp speed when you turn over this compact timepiece. Also ideal for games of Pictionary and charades below deck.
$15.00

Oddi Shirts
Want to look Icelandic? So do we.
$20.00

Striped Socks

A little known key to successful plunder: calf definition. Also good for extra dagger storage.

$7.00

Powder Horns

Styles: Brass, wood, or marble. Frequency of sale: 3 per month (7 per day during Local Militia Discount Week). Most common questions/remarks: "Is this the same as a flagon, and if not, where can I find potential flagons?" For the younger pirates, we recommend the powder horn for use as a canteen or Pixie Stix receptacle.

Brass: $25.00   Wood: $28.00   Marble: $35.00

Taxi Horns

Style: Loud and bulbous. Most common questions/remarks: "My, that's loud. And bulbous, too." Frankly, we prefer it that way. Anyone who says that pirates should be seen and not heard doesn't know his earring from his eyepatch.

$17.00

Bugles

Style: Copper with handy screw-on cap. Frequency of sale: 1 per fortnight.

$22.00

Horseshoes

For hurling in exhibition of agility and strength, for shooting from cannons, for melting down and recasting as artillery, and, we suppose, for equipping horses.

$5.00

Snake Boxes
Not only are they perfect for startling the neurotic, these boxes also house the only reptilian pets guaranteed to answer when you call.
$5.00

Regular Stock:

Eyepatches
Want to plunder with pizzazz? Tired of that unsightly black cloth covering your empty eye socket? Even the most grizzled of pirates will be titillated by our new primary and pastel collections.
$4.00

Pirate Flags
Including Bartholomew Roberts, Jack Rackham, Edward Teach, Jolly Roger, and Christopher Moody. Each pirate had his own insignia flag with its own meaning. Guess which one means "Your time is running out?"
Small: $11.00   Medium: $13.00   Large: $22.00

Skull Soap
A delightful vanilla scent for the days you don't really feel like walking the plank.
$6.00

We also have on hand, in no particular order: old and new charts, wax seals, swordsmen shirts, pirate perfumes and other rare essences, glass eyes, peg legs, and lard. Many of our sundries can be purchased online. Please visit www.826valencia.org/store/.

Staff Picks:

The Five Hundred Year Calendar Paper Weight

"If you buy a calendar every year, you're spending ten dollars each time. That's five thousand dollars over the next five hundred years! This perfectly weighted calendar is so economical, it actually pays you to use it."   —K. Petty

Lard

"It's not all about lubrication, but increasingly, I find that things roll along better with lard. One day I accidentally dropped my bicycle in the lardbucket, and since then, you can hardly see me when I pedal past. Partly for the same reason, I've been larding all things that need to be faster or seen less. The other part of the reason is that lard is a no-fail friendmaker. Touch someone with lard, and they're your friend... forever."   —A. Villanueva

Books and Publications

In addition to these pirate supplies, we also sell publications written by our students:

826 Quarterly Vol. 1

826 Quarterly Vol. 2

Talking Back: What Students Know about Teaching

Waiting to Be Heard: Youth Speak Out about Inheriting a Violent World

2 lbs. of Short Stories

A Poem Is Worth a Thousand Pictures

A Poem for Each Blade of Grass

Blue As 5 Birds

Glass over Dynamite

Looking 4 It

Read This!

Starzen's Booty and Other Stories, *by Phoebe Morgan*

[Straight-Up News], with news from Everett Middle School

The Book of Many Names

The Book with No Name

The Fifth Grade Tiny Tigers' Literary Magazine

What It Is.

McSweeney's related books can also be purchased.

Store Log

On any given day, odd things happen. Especially here. Sometimes, they are planned, other days not. The following has been excerpted from our log which accounts real events that have occurred in our shop:

3/23/04
"Every Last One"
Today, all of Portland was here.

5/6/04
"An Educational Joke"
Q: Why does lightning never learn anything?
A: Because it always has its head in the clouds.

6/10/04
"Lard Trivia"
Patsy is an expert on lice and lard. She sent us the following report:

Lard is used to kill head lice in some southern areas of this wide country of ours. It is a little messy to get out of really long, thin hair; the hot water sometimes scalds the person attached to the hair. It is much safer than the other remedy of head lice removal, kerosene. Even unlit, it burns the skin if left on long enough to actually kill the lice.

Lard is a last ditch effort, after Nix, Rid and store brands have done nothing other than make the head lice stronger, more virulent and better groomed than the head lice of the person who gave them to you.

In exchange for her information, Patsy would like the answer to this question: how many pounds of lard are rendered from one three hundred pound hog?

Let us know if you have the answer.

6/14/04
"Joke Potpourri"

Several jokes from bartering children:

"Call cheese, which is not your cheese, nacho cheese."

"A skeleton walks into a bar and says, 'Gimme a beer. And a mop.'"

"Q: What kind of turtle never goes blind?"
"A: A sea turtle."

6/18/04
"Sadness"

Our fish that we called The Eel (although it was technically a fish, not an eel) has passed. His death wasn't pretty. Hermit crabs have a rather particular way of showing their respect for the dead.

Julia was quite moved by this sudden loss from the fish theater, and she has made a large series of messages in bottles regarding this important issue.

6/21/04
"For Cousin Bradley"

A patron recently announced, "Eagles may soar high, but weasels don't get sucked into jet engines."

6/24/04
"Disgust Disguised"

Our shopkeepers are often on the receiving end of unsolicited confessions. An individual recently divulged that he had once prepared a block of lard for a company potluck. With the addition of a few sprigs of parsley, it was disguised as cheese.

Store Thanks:

We would like to thank all of the store workers for their continued support and dedication:

Tim Anderson, Caitlin Craven, Tika Hall, Suzanne Kleid, Amie Nenninger, and Julia White.

Store Hours:

Open 12–6 p.m. every day.
826 Valencia St.
San Francisco, CA 94110
www.826valencia.org/store

Come by the store for a free mopping!